The Dark Legend of the Foreigner

The Dark Legend of the Foreigner

Frank DeStefano

LifeRich
PUBLISHING

LifeRich Publishing is a registered trademark of
The Reader's Digest Association, Inc.

LifeRich Publishing books may be ordered
through booksellers or by contacting:

LifeRich Publishing
1663 Liberty Drive
Bloomington, IN 47403
www.liferichpublishing.com
1 (888) 238-8637

ISBN: 978-1-4897-0157-2 (sc)
ISBN: 978-1-4897-0158-9 (e)

Print information available on the last page.

LifeRich Publishing rev. date: 11/08/2019

Chapter 1

It had been years since there was anything close to a normal way of life in Japan. There had been many changes to Japan in the 17th century.

The year was 1605, and Japan was hit by the effects of a devastating earthquake and tsunami at around 8 p.m. on February 3, 1605. The earthquake had a magnitude of 7.9 on the surface, which triggered a devasting tsunami. It was higher than expected, given the projections.

There had been thousands and thousands of deaths in the four regions that had been affected. Along with deaths of people, 700 homes were destroyed, many castles were completely destroyed, and others had severe damage that would take years to rebuild, since at that time they didn't have the supplies and things used in more modern eras. There were 5,000 that were killed during this event.

But Japan was in a world completely by itself and in a different period of time than the rest of the world. The devastations were hard to imagine, as areas were completely destroyed, people in the thousands were left dead. Animals, people were wiped out in a matter of seconds. It was nature raging against a way of living. There was nothing that anyone could have done to prevent such a life-changing event that led to so much destruction.

The regions that had suffered the most damage—that word could not come close to describing the destruction—were the Chuba region, Kansa Region, Shikokus region, and the Kyushu region.

The southern coast of Honshu runs parallel to the Nankai Trough. It marks the subduction of the Philippine Sea, beneath the Eurasian Plate. Not too far from there was a town called Okla, which had felt the tsunami worst of all, as it destroyed and killed many in that disaster. It was a booming town where families had lived and settled and farmed and done the things that most families had done in order to survive. All the rural area had been destroyed and had been left flooded for what seemed like years and years, and never seemed to be the same ever again from that one moment in history. As time passed, it had been difficult for many to even begin to go back or attempt to return to see what had become of their homes, and how bad the destruction was in Okla. The idea of attempting such a thing was dreadful. It was very painful to look at an area and understand how your town was destroyed by nature. Not one person would be able to stomach something that so fundamentally changed their very existence.

There were so many things that weren't going right in the very early 1600s. That was one thing that held in many beliefs in so many things. How would the people in these areas survive? They had no roof over their head, no shelter from wild animals or anything in Japan. The castles that ruled over the people were destroyed or washed away. The land was in ruins, and nothing left for the people to live on or for. Some had survived, and others had the opportunity to get far enough away from the regions that the tsunami hit the hardest. There had been some in spurts as some people had come back, but why would they? That would be the greatest question.

It is something that we do as humans; we tend to go back to what we know and things to which we have formed attachments. It is in human nature to go to what we know best. So many things had changed in that span of time and years. A whole rebuilding process of Okla, and the shoguns had been completely wiped out and a rebuilding period begun from every way—from rebuilding an army to rebuilding the area that seemingly had to begin anew.

The Japanese people knew how to survive and learned how to adapt to the things that were presented to them. It was a very bleak picture that had consumed them with things that were near impossible to think about. There were more questions than answers. Shattered homes, and pieces that had scattered across the beach and the land, from the four regions where broken lives had been destroyed. You often saw the heartbreak of the people and the surrounding areas. Any given person felt the heartbreak and the loss of life, young or old, newborn and others. You felt the heartache from so many angles.

The rulers in the castles had been killed, and even the seventh wizard had died. Rincewind was dressed in his yellow cloak and his balding head. In months before, his time was nearing at a competition held in honor of the emperor Tashbi. Radagast, the seventh wizard, had seen young apprentices who seemed eager to learn the world of magic and become his replacements. As the seventh wizard, he had consulted the ponytailed emperor, and after killing his father, he blamed it on his sister, as he had set her up and pinned the death on her.

Months before the tsunami, Emperor Tashbi had let the ultimate abuse of power come over him. He had ordered the beheading of his only sister. He knew the truth and felt no remorse about his actions. Tashbi's father had run a simple but peaceful empire. He was one of the rare ones, and under his rule, most shoguns and people had gotten along. But, Tashbi's view was filled with nothing but death and destruction. It had followed the many emperors before him. Tashbi's father was rare, but Tashbi himself was the ultimate. However, his view of death, and with that, his rule, didn't last long, only a matter of months.

The seventh wizard, Rincewind, who lived in the castle with Emperor Tashbi, was aging. Secretly, away from the castle, he had done something the six other wizards of time had never done. He had brought him to the most forbidden place, the place only dead or retired wizards had gone. Radagast, the new trainee, was young and full of life and innocence. He had been training for the most powerful position. Over months and years, Rincewind had taught him, and the time would soon come when both of them would leave earth and go to the Temple of Time, a forbidden act that the other six wizards of the realm were very much against. Each one's power was very different from the other's. Rincewind had seen many things and was trying to tell them of Okla's destruction, but it was more than what he and others could understand.

As he stood in the battle room, the other six wizards took quite a different approach. They were incredulous and could not believe what he had said to the others around the magical realm in the Temple of Time. Where they stood seemed like a completely different place, and a very unfamiliar area. The other six wizards stood bickering at Rincewind and all his reasoning at the big table. They all protested, as though their reasoning was better than Rincewind's offering.

But Rincewind was able to see far past the future, as he moved his hands from left to right, and opened what seemed like a white magic cloud. He was able to reveal the events and timeline of the different things that had transpired, and how they had happened. It was Rincewind who had pleaded with the magical wizards in the Temple of Time. He knew, and when you believe in something so strongly, you both believe it and feel it as well. That was how Rincewind showed the six wizards that surrounded the magic realm table. They all sat around and even now they looked at each other, still unwilling to believe him.

They saw every event that had occurred. Rincewind had showed them in the air, and a temple of magic and mystery of everything would float, everything and anything that you could imagine. From magical books to a book of spells. A bookcase that stretched to the ceiling and even beyond that.

Rincewind stood on the open seal of the Wizard Realm and pleaded as he held his hands tightly together, begging for mercy, and he looked at each of them as he wished for hope. He seemed to be the last hope, the one hope that his country and others still had. Each different wizard and each cloak that they wore had sat around the table, and each color had represented something different. As they all had their specialty in something that was so unique and so much more powerful than the next one.

Rincewind looked at them and waved his magic all around them, vanishing them all to what was an image, and placing them directly in what he had tried to show them, but which they had refused to see or believe. As Rincewind stood behind them with Radagast, he didn't know what to think. He was so young, and he was the last of a long line of generational wizards: the eight wizards of the Temple of Time. As there were eight chairs, they constructed this oversized large table, which had spells and everything else you could imagine. But it also had a book containing the things in time that were controlled by the Temple of Time, and details about how and why this temple existed. They each had a large part of history and had played a role in saving it from many crucial events, good and bad, over the periods of time. It was a way of controlling the balance in the world wherever they were needed. Rincewind, in his yellow cloak, seemingly was third-most powerful to the others, and he was shocked that he had done that to all the others.

As he looked at all of them, and Rincewind called his young apprentice, he felt something building up, and he was fighting for him, as he had a gift of every wizard within his magic and power. It could have possibly been the reason why the others were so afraid of seeing what he himself believed in giving Radagast the red cloak.

The red cloak was the most powerful of them all. The first wizard wore blue, and others wore different colors, never the same. Radagast had listened and believed everything that Rincewind had said and showed the others. "There is a war coming and that war will bring forward death and turmoil in ways that you can't believe. I am seeing this, and I feel the pains and suffering on a daily basis. There are things I will show you," he said as he talked to all of them.

"We see what you are doing," the blue wizard had answered with his longest beard, as he was the most powerful. "We will not be influenced by your mind power and powerful thoughts."

Rapidly, he snapped them back from the Temple of Time to the board room.

"No!" Rincewind yelled, as he realized, based on their current surroundings in Okla, compared to what they'd seen, this event was to happen almost twenty-five years into the future. It was scheduled for the year 1650: the birth of The Master.

As Rincewind stood, he froze time for them all. He thought that if it was going to be that way, then the Temple of Time was to become a real temple somewhere that would never be found, in the deep part of the Amazon rainforest.

Rincewind froze them, walking slowly, cursing them and cursing himself as he aged so quickly. Soon he became a frozen statue among the temple, which would later become a piece of art work in the temple, along with many other pictures on the wall.

His body crumbled to dust, and as the dust swirled away, the wind picked up his last words. "Don't let him ever live…"

Rincewind's passion inspired something even greater, as Radagast felt he had to win the competition that Emperor Tashbi had set for the kingdom. There was something about the passion that he had, and there was something that had lured him even more. The things Rincewind had shown Radagast were going to be used as a greater source and a greater power for him. His life would not last as long as the others, but being as one of the more powerful wizards he would be, he would be part of something hundreds of years into the future. Radagast had accepted this truth and believed he was the right man for the job as well. It was something he would not back down from. He knew who and what he was and what needed to be done.

#

After Radagast teleported himself back, his return made it seem as if he were gone for months. Yet it had only seemed like days to him. In fact, it was much longer, nearly four months having passed. By the time he had returned, Emperor Tashbi had sent out a search party for his yellow cloaked wizard.

He went into the kingdom and approached the guards that were near. He asked to speak with them, but a lot of them were very hesitant to do so. Looking around, he whispered a spell and moved all of the guards forcibly away, throwing them into the wall that wasn't far from where he stood. Frightened, they agreed to his request. They knew that Emperor Tashbi had been looking for the seventh wizard, and as Emperor Tashbi had been looking for the yellow cloaked wizard, there seemingly was no sign of him until this moment.

As he regarded the emperor and began to approach him, he sensed that there was great trouble. The red cloaked wizard knelt before the emperor and took off his red hat. He was very young to be this powerful, the emperor mused as he looked at him.

"Stand up," Emperor Tashbi commanded the wizard.

As he listened, and as he noticed how things were different, he wondered if maybe it was much more time that he had been gone. Radagast couldn't remember how much time had passed. Maybe the Temple of Time messed with his brain on how much time had gone by as well. He couldn't understand what really happened, and why Rincewind had fought so hard for him, the apprentice he had taken under his wing from a very violent upbringing. Rincewind had killed his parents to save Radagast from a brutal death. That was something that he had to do, a moral obligation. So Radagast had been more than grateful for a gesture in return. Rincewind had saved his life and from the very early age of 10, he had been training him since.

As Radagast approached the emperor, he knew something was up. The emperor had ordered him to kill all the other wizards that challenged him. He had ordered all the others and had a horn blown for a wizard battle.

Everyone realized what was happening, as they walked outside towards the castle. Emperor Tashbi had told Radagast to rise to his feet and follow him to the battle ground. The emperor didn't believe that he was simply given the red cloak. He thought that he had killed for it, just the way that he had killed his sister as well.

"You would now," he responded and smirked.

The emperor grabbed him and slammed him against one of the large pillars that held the castle together.

Radagast was a bit of a wise guy as well. He smiled and looked at him. "The truth lies with me, as I know everything about you."

Instantaneously, Radagast was grabbed by the emperor and plowed right through the people in his castle. As his approached his throne room, he slammed the door shut and the guards were positioned right outside the door. They asked if he needed them inside the room.

"No!" he answered with a booming, angry voice that they all understood.

Radagast walked around with his cloak on and his robe closed, his hands closed as he walked around. His arrogance and cockiness were more convincing to the emperor through his actions and body language. That was something that made him respectful of him. He saw himself in the young wizard, and he liked that. The fact that he had recognized such tendencies in Radagast assured him that his relationship with the new, powerful wizard would be a long-lasting one, and not one that would cloud his judgment at all. The emperor wanted supreme power to destroy anyone or anything who believed in his rule or not. Radagast would make a fine ally, he thought to himself.

As Radagast looked into his eyes, he saw what he was going to do within time. As he had said, the destruction of this land would take years to rebuild, from 1605 and the tsunami that had killed thousands. He saw everything that the new emperor was going to do, and Radagast had no choice but to let things fall into place the way that Rincewind had told him they were going to happen. There was no saving him from anything the emperor was going to do. The destruction would come and the people would see the things that he had seen, all in due course.

"I will support you in anything you do," he said as he bowed towards him. "You are my emperor." He kneeled before him on the wet gravel of the castle and waved his two arms.

"Stand up," the emperor told him.

Radagast stood slowly and brushed the dirt off his knees. He smiled. "You must do what you have to do as well."

The emperor smiled, and without saying much, both of them knew that the one secret that Emperor Tashbi had tried to hide, the eighth wizard, Radagast, had known. He was careful not to say anything that would make him think too deeply about it. Radagast had chosen his words very wisely. In the end, they both smiled and they both shook each other's hands. As they performed this gesture, the undercurrent between them was palpable. Were they both shaking each other's hand as they were shaking it with the devil? That remained to be seen.

Radagast the red cloaked wizard, the eighth and final one, had constructed the Temple of Time realm. He knew things had to be the way that they were transpiring. His time would be short, but it was in that time that he had everything to fall to him, and in the end, he would become what Rincewind the seventh wizard was, the one who saw the greatness and the fall of the world. Something that he made sure that Radagast would be able to see and understand as well. He took it to heart as well. It was something beyond his control, and he was told never to change things in the end.

Emperor Tashbi walked out with his armor in place. The faces that appeared on his armor represented the descendants of the kingdom who had ruled and protected it. As one of the few castles in the region that hadn't been completely destroyed by the massive tsunami, they had years of work to do to rebuild and to get the people back. The castle, as much as they had wanted the town of Okla, was something that would not work for them. Radagast advised him that this would never work. It seemed the emperor had a decision to make, and he would make it after the true test of the wizard.

They departed the throne room together, and walked out into the open yard, where the battle ground was being set up by the emperor's guards. The crowd was sparse, as most of the people had either moved on from the great disaster or died. The destruction was evident, as most things were all over, weapons and other debris strewn about from the massive destruction. As the emperor had known in his heart, it would take a miracle to live and survive in Okla. It was in ruins, and there was nothing left in it. Why should anyone stay if there wasn't anything that was left for them to live for?

As Emperor Tashbi, with his long ponytail, looked around, and saw everything that was in shambles, he contemplated that he had to convince them that Okla was dead, and what was once a booming town was now a desolate town with no life, and if there were any lives left, they would soon die. A town with hundreds of families, which stretched for about fifteen miles, and houses set along the ways, it was more populated than any town along the coast of the Shikoku Region. Okla wasn't far from the mountains, as it had an entrance up and the same entrance down. A water source wasn't too far from it either. This was the source that had destroyed the town.

The emperor had asked any of the training wizards to step forward as they all lined up to do battle as had been requested of them. Even Radagast stood with his red cloak. He knew what he wanted.

The emperor cast his eyes on them and waved before the others could say anything or attempt a more powerful spell on him, which would be highly unlikely, but he didn't want to take any chances. He noted that Radagast, the young-looking wizard, for the most part had no facial hair and was lucky he had enough hair to wear the red hat that he had donned.

Just then, Radagast snapped both his fingers, and the challengers exploded, all eight of them. Blood went flying all over from the other apprentices that stood in the yard waiting to attempt to win and become the emperor's wizard.

The emperor surveyed the scene before him, including the guards and some of the people who stood covered in blood from what had been done to them. It was extremely gruesome and it looked as if pints of blood were everywhere, and covered from head to toe, from the people that remained in the kingdom to the guards. The Emperor was taken aback by the turn of events. It wasn't something that he had thought of, or ever would have imagined to show how vicious he could be. That's what the wizard had said to Emperor Tashbi in his throne room. He had to prove it, and Radagast had done just that. He had made his point regarding how seriously he would take being loyal. The Emperor liked brutal and painful death. He showed him, while the Emperor made all wizards compete for his loyalty, and he did something so brutal that no one could come close. The way he'd done it, with two snaps of his fingers, making everyone explode one by one was brutal. The blood. The bones and body parts going all over, and whatever organs remained flying into the crowd. It was something that he liked and enjoyed, evident by his smile.

The emperor now knew what a vicious wizard he had in his power, a killing machine. In the years to come, with his help, they would cause something greater than Japan had ever seen.

As that day came to an end, time was headed in a direction that surely revealed how the world at that time had been changing.

#

Radagast eventually found a place to sleep. There wasn't much left of one of the few castles that hadn't been washed away from the water that crashed upon the shore. He had looked around and lay with the rotting animals that had been slaughtered and were destroyed from animals that had managed to survive. There were smells that the human nose couldn't stomach or ponder what it might be either. There was too much going on, and the life that been destroyed was something far greater than what the true cause of everything was.

Emperor Tashbi had his own intentions. He, too, knew that from what he viewed and how he needed to come into power was by building his army. He also knew that this would take time, much more so than some might think. After such a crushing blow to that area of Okla, and losing almost 5,000 people between the four regions, it made it so terrible and devasting to all areas. It was like starting all over from something or bringing a new time to something. As the kingdom had less than fifty people, compared to what was once the booming town of Okla, Radagast knew that even though it had to happen eventually, no one in their right frame of mind would come back to where destruction had occurred. That was one thing that most people wouldn't think twice about. Finding places to sleep were hard, as it was cold, damp, and wet, and even for most to find shelter, not to mention the things that would possibly threaten them, made it harder to wonder what could happen, what harm could befall them, while their eyes would be shut at night.

But the emperor wondered, not about his people, but rather how his army could grow and how much more dominating he could be. He could become one of the most powerful emperors of his time and be the baldest one of them all, a distinction that would set him apart. With great power, the sky was the limit for him, and with Radagast as his right-hand man, there wasn't anything or anyone that would deter him or tell him no. The rise and fall would be his own undoing, and that was something he couldn't and wouldn't control either. While most had searched for places to sleep, the emperor didn't help any of them in their search, as he wanted the people to figure it out. That wasn't his problem.

He had to move away from Okla and that was his concern. Where could he go?

Emperor Tashbi had a few of his soldiers that remained, in the destroyed castle. He looked out into a mist of the land that was covered in a thick fog. He wasn't sure what to do, and, as many people before him, he was following in the same footsteps. He wanted death and total destruction.

Radagast wasn't too far away. He had traversed the wet, soiled land in order to try to help some of the scattered people find someplace dry and warm, which was extremely hard to do. There had been bales of hay that, just looking around, seemed like the warmest place for those people he had seen alive. They had lacked food, water, and supplies to live.

Radagast spent the next few hours toiling, trying to help the people survive another day. Finally, he stood up, after he had reunited some of the children with their mothers and fathers, if they had survived, which in some cases they hadn't. He had to find others who would take them under their wing. It was heartbreaking, and whatever warmth he could provide for them, he took upon him as his duty, as he knew the emperor didn't care one bit about anything like that at all. To him, it was all about power and control over the people and the land, and that was all that mattered, whether anyone liked it or not.

Radagast had walked for a bit with a walking stick that fit perfectly, even though he was the youngest to be appointed a wizard by the emperor. He glanced back over all of the destruction he had walked through, strewn about the whole area. He had walked for nearly an hour, and he had reached a point in Okla that intrigued him, as Rincewind had seen and told Radagast that his death would take him to Okla It was the town that he was currently in, and a destroyed town, too.

Slowly, he approached the area that Rincewind had revealed to him in his visions; it was somewhere he had to go. Radagast, against Rincewind's wishes and warnings to the contrary, resolved to press onward. It was something that he had to do for his own piece of mind.

He emerged from the destroyed nature forest, or what was left of it. There were patches here and there, and practically no trees. It was mostly dirt and some grassy patches, and a lot of water buildups along the path he took had walked. But it was very dark and gloomy where he had walked to. It wasn't the large town he was used to, and just looking around, he saw as much, if not more, damage as he had seen from the castle area. It was practically unimaginable. But he saw animals dead, people dead, hundreds of destroyed houses and farm lands—there was nothing there.

As he looked around, turning his head in all directions, the sights were equally dismal, no matter where he looked. Dark, as if Hell itself had taken over. The Okla mountains were a few miles south of where he had approached a hut. It had looked like the weakest thing that he had seen, standing. But how could it even stand when all the other surrounding homes and things were completely destroyed from the tsunami? He couldn't understand it.

Radagast walked towards it, crossing into a territory that was well beyond where he should have been. It was something that Rincewind had strongly advised him not to ever do. Radagast, however, was headstrong and didn't listen to his mentor.

As he advanced, he started to see flashes of images, things that Rincewind had seen. A war that would stir up years later, and from that, a great evil that would rise. He saw all the horrific images, of death and destruction, and along with them, one man and one person named "The Master." Just as the images of destruction began, they were quickly cut off; he wasn't meant to see so much.

Radagast fell to the muddy soil in front of the hut. He couldn't fully comprehend the images he had seen. But the warrior in his vision looked fierce and mean. The Master. With a skull as a face, and red eyes, he was a warrior much more intact than anything he had seen before. It terrified him, and he quickly backed away from the hut. As he pushed his hands through the mud as fast as he could, there was something about the hut that he saw he could get into. But that was clearly not the case. It was like something was magical about the place or was something that Rincewind the magical wizard had done; or else, he knew that Radagast would go there after telling him, after seeing the images that Rincewind had shown the other six wizards from the Temple of Time.

As Radagast had his hands and feet caked in the mud, his heart raced extremely fast and scared the life out of him as he continued to back away. He attempted to slow his breaths, unable to shake the residual feelings from seeing things that he shouldn't have. But, seeing the images that Rincewind had shown the other wizards from the Temple of Time, he found that it was much more powerful to feel the images, then see the images as well. It was something that was more difficult to feel. It was stressful and gave him anxiety to a point that made him confused about what he was feeling. But, for Radagast, it was a bit of many different things all at once. He couldn't quite understand what those emotions were either. It overwhelmed him.

He had gradually gotten to his feet, and he thought about what he felt and saw. Now, he was worried. This was what Rincewind had been talking about, that his destiny had already been written for him, and the sacrifice that he was going to make later years in life was preordained.

The words echoed in his brain as he stood up with his walking stick. He was in his early 40's at best. All the other previous wizards had lived for hundreds and hundreds of years through times of turmoil and changing events. It was what Rincewind knew would be his ultimate sacrifice, and, being the much more powerful red wizard of the rest of the seven previous wizards, he knew it was his duty to make things better, though time and events he could not change.

Radagast walked back toward the direction he came from, and as he did, he could have sworn he heard laughter—a very evil laugh. He wasn't dreaming or imagining things. He knew he had heard something, but he didn't know where it had come from. It was something evil, that he had sensed, and a much more evil presence than he had ever known about. It was something on top of what he began to know was something mysterious. A loud voice that covered the land and an echo that couldn't be unknown to the land. This made him even more worried, as things of this nature terrified him to a level that he couldn't understand at this point.

#

By early morning, Radagast had finally gotten back to where the castle was. He looked at the sky and couldn't understand how the sun had been replaced by clouds. It was Okla had been cursed, with no trace of sunlight or any light whatsoever. It had made Radagast wonder what and where he had just been. What was Okla? At least that part of it seemed completely separate from the early parts where the castle was? He couldn't completely understand, and he wouldn't until the time came to do so.

As he returned to what was left of the castle, he searched for Emperor Tashbi. Radagast had walked up the broken castle stairways very carefully and watched the cracks in the stairs, as there were many that had been damaged from the tsumani.

He finally reached Emperor Tashbi, walking over and around the damage's debris from the castle and broken fragments that had blocked some doors and rooms. Radagast was the youngest of all the wizards, which made him better equipped to jump and use his agility to his advantage. When he finally got to where Emperor Tashbi was, he looked at him and kneeled before him, then stood up again.

"It is time to move," he said solemnly. "It is going to be safe for the people."

For once, Tashbi had agreed. This was no place to build an army of any kind. While Tashbi saw something, Radagast saw something opposite. Their visions were aligned, but Radagast had seen something that was completely beyond what he had wanted to see. It was a sign of something or something quite out of the ordinary but served as a warning of things that would occur. From his short stature, Emperor

Tashbi examined Radagast, covered in mud, his cloak that was usually red stained brown from the wet and soft soil that was in Okla.

"What happened?" Emperor Tashbi asked.

Radagast went on to tell him with a smile how he went exploring to see what he would find, and he had fallen into some soft spots with mud in them. The emperor had laughed seeing him, and he made fun of his story, and of all the dried mud all over his red cloak.

Radagast brushed off what remaining dirt he had on himself. He smiled and they both laughed. It was time, the emperor said. Time to move on, like he was told to by Radagast.

Tashbi had gathered his people where the top of the castle used to be. It had been destroyed from the tsunami, and most of the top part of the castle was missing. Tashbi had called, and they all asked what was left of the courtyard, where they all stood when he would call the people to listen to him speak.

They stood and looked up to him. He looked around and the few people that had remained looked at him with a glimmer of hope and survival instinct. As they listened, the emperor told them it was time to move on. It was what most of them wanted to hear. From what he had seen looking down at the people, the conditions of the way of life were worse than any conditions that peasants had to live in. There was some hope now, as Radagast had given Tashbi. At some point, he had to get the shoguns involved somehow, to show him what he needed to do. Sometimes it was the only way that he was able to see what he truly wanted to see. Tashbi had his own intentions that were far greater than anything he had thought about along the line. There was truly no comparison to anything else, either.

The people had cheered a bit at the emperor's proclamation, and Radagast smiled as he stood next to the armored emperor. He said, "I think they are starting to like you a bit."

Emperor Tashbi smiled and laughed. "I guess I can't make a habit of that?" he said. It was something that they both laughed about a few times.

The people of Okla were given 24 hours to pack whatever things they had. It was the only way to give them enough time to find anything they had left. It was understandably the right thing to do. As Radagast had told him, it was the wise thing to do as well. Not that he was all about doing the right thing, as Tashbi was more about himself and building up the shogun army once they had found a safe place to rebuild. Those was his intentions, and they were very strong ones.

"Are you coming?" asked Tashbi as he walked away.

Radagast responded that he wasn't. He needed some time to think about things. As he stood on one of the broken stones that had been split in the castle, one of many that existed throughout the castle, he looked up at the sky and pondered, as he so often did, what voice, and what future he signed up for. At the time, he wanted to be great, but he did not realize the sacrifices or the way his future would be written long before the years would approach.

#

The next morning, he had still been up on the same rock. He appeared to be a statue of some sort. Tashbi saw him in the same spot as he had left him. He almost looked like he was praying, but he wasn't at all. It was his way of thinking. There were so many things that had to get done. The emperor had assembled most of the people, and now he had looked for Radagast, finding him in the same area where he had left him.

"Are you okay?" he smiled. Radagast knew that despite how ruthless as he was acting and his intentions being very evident, he seemed to care about Radagast. But this was merely a guess.

As it was time to head out, the emperor waved his hand to come down from where he stood on the remnants of the castle. It seemed as if there was really now more hope for them, and a better place awaited them, away from Okla and this decaying and destroyed castle. Radagast knew this and yet he felt fearful that the next time he would be there would possibly be his last. But he realized it was part of his destiny as well.

He looked back at Emperor Tashbi as he walked away from Radagast and headed towards where the people waited for their emperor. As he turned his head, the emperor yelled in his native Japanese language and waved his hands for him to come towards him.

He smiled, knowing it was going to be a place that he would not see for many years, and soon, Okla was going to be a far-off land. But that time would go by quickly, as he had given it one last look of fate that would be met. It was only 1605, and there were many more years to go.

As he answered his emperor and headed away, he bowed towards the town, knowing that his fate was written. Knowing all the things that the seventh wizard had showed him, he was more accepting of it at this point. He had realized that there was a higher plan of attack to some degree.

Radagast followed the emperor towards where the people had waited for him to be at his side. He cast one final look at everything and smiled. He then went with Emperor Tashbi.

He followed his careful footing over the cracks in the stone, and the pieces of pillars and stone that had begun to shake loose from the castle, making it seemingly unsteady. With the way the structure had fallen, and the precarious way the things leaned against each other, it was only a matter of time.

Emperor Tashbi had ordered his soldiers to search the broken castle for anyone who had possibly wandered off to places that they couldn't escape from. It wasn't like they had many people to leave the group. It was simply going to be the best way forward they could possibly have.

The emperor finally decided it was beyond the right thing to do. He had gathered and waited for all the guards to come back, as he had counted the number of soldiers that he had, along with all their weapons. He hadn't really known what to expect from what was out there. Some of the people were afraid of what could be awaiting them. Others were afraid of what could have been if they had stayed at the castle as well. There wasn't much that would happen that would be good. A battle of things that could possibly attack as far as wild animals were concerned. The survival rate for them was less and less with each passing day. That was the one thing that they all could agree on. They all needed to survive to each new day, as Radagast had to convince Emperor Tashbi as well. He knew that all the things Radagast had said had always made sense, and a 40-year-old wizard was by far one of the youngest wizards, and also one of the wisest with common sense as well.

As they headed out of that area for the last time, they had gotten the few remaining stragglers that had crept away for some reason or another. As the emperor had seen, they had taken a few of the lost treasures from the castle and wanted to use it for trade to get supplies that they needed as well.

Radagast looked on, as the emperor instructed the soldiers to hold them. The two guards of his fallen and destroyed kingdom walked along the broken debris, plants, and trees, and moved much farther away from everything. They had gone much more inland, far away from an area where this could ever happen again, they hoped. It had been about a half day's trip, and they finally came to an area that had some life to it, and a castle that looked deserted, as if nothing had been there for about twenty years or so.

Radagast, searching alongside the emperor, saw a machine that was built to behead people. The two soldiers saw that there were numerous of these guillotines in front of the castle. When they saw them, the emperor told the soldiers to put the two thieves there, as the soldiers had sorted out the criminals.

He looked fiercely out at the people and said, "No one steals from me."

The soldiers swiftly placed them in the machine. Their heads were locked away, along with their hands, through a piece of wood. It looked impossible to get out, and there were chains to lock them in. The wood was all covered in dried red blood.

As he spoke to his people, he took out his sword, as the emperor had done. He walked over towards each of them, and he cut off their heads one by one. Emperor Tashbi had no mercy and didn't care about people who stole or did things against him. He stood before a castle, his people, and what was left from the tsunami that had destroyed the lives of so many. He stood in front of a castle and called it home. It appeared to have been deserted for what seemed like years now. It was now Castle Alanga in Shizuoka, Japan.

Chapter 2

There hadn't been many people that were left from the tsunami. Emperor Tashbi stood there with Radagast, having found the castle, and he saw less than fifty people who had dragged their things. He knew that there were many things that he had wondered and thought about, as he had seen the great destruction over the years. The red cloaked wizard had much to learn. But he had also gained so much knowledge, as he was far more powerful than any others that had come before, given his power and seeing what he had seen. His power was far greater than any of the other wizards before him.

As he followed in the footsteps of the evil and twisted Emperor Tashbi, he had seen the destruction of many over the years and just complete chaos. His ideas of power and destruction were far greater than he had believed. The emperor was obsessed with destruction and death. Even if anyone had looked at him funny, it would be beheading for them and nothing less.

Radagast had seen everything that was going to happen. It was scary, as he knew he was going to be involved in everything that he had seen—all the bad, and not too much good. Each day, more and more people had scattered and eventually came out for a place to live and survive. There were so many things that the emperor had seen and not for the best. As months and months had gone by, it had been almost a year, and the kingdom had grown and grown, the population booming, the army growing, along with the weapons. The learning of its agriculture growth and many other things that had made a kingdom function as well all began to take shape.

It had been at least five years since the great tsunami had happened. The emperor had been in almost an extinct faction. The wizard stood and was in a wooded area, as the emperor and Radagast had been safe from any natural disaster. Radagast had sentenced something, and he knew things would be starting, as the whole process of things would take time, just like anything.

Shichiro, a young 16-year-old warrior, came out from the bushes. The emperor stood and saw him covered in blood from head to toe. He smiled as he stood in front of the emperor, and he heard the footsteps of many following him.

As he got beyond the grass area, the emperor's men came running behind him. The wizard and the emperor saw from about 100 yards away that Shichiro had blood all over him, and not much skin that was seen and sword in hand. As the emperor watched, twelve men ran out from the wooded area. They had him surrounded. They all looked at each other.

He told him where he was from and why he was there. This child had killed his six brothers, his mother, and his father.

Emperor Tashbi smiled and laughed. He looked at him, as the child had a look of death and destruction on his face. He responded to the leading shogun, "Proceed if you can."

Apparently, his family couldn't take him down, as the shogun had said they would, and the emperor looked and gestured to him to go ahead, that he would see if he could.

Shichiro, the Japanese warrior, was surrounded by twelve shoguns. He paced back and forth and didn't know which way to look, but he kept a keen eye on every which way as much as he could.

His eyes were laser focused and he could smell the fear of the shoguns that stood in front of him. Shichiro, being such a young warrior, didn't have much of a build but was still a skilled and effective warrior, as he was from one of the well-known shogun clans in Japan. His clan was one of the most feared as well. His family had generations and generations of men who would continue his name. He was one of the Lees.

Radagast was well aware of who he was, too, to an even greater extent than the emperor or the shoguns. He sat back and watched things happen as he knew it had to happen, and he couldn't alter the timeline of things. He knew it would alter not just the history of Japan but the whole world. Even though Radagast had known nothing outside the world of Japan, he figured there was so much more beyond the water that had surrounded Japan.

As the emperor took particular interest in the way that Radagast stared at him, he fixed an intense gaze back at him. Radagast hadn't taken his eyes off of him, as though he had smelled fear. His eyes were in a trance that conveyed he had known something much greather than what he was letting on, compared to what the emperor had known. It was something that Emperor Tashbi had innately felt. That was one of the main reasons he didn't kill the warrior, as he could have when he was right in front of him. There was something that the emperor had felt in many ways as well, intuitively.

As they continued to stare each other down, both knew he was special over the other. It was what Radagast had really known much more than what the emperor had really known. Radagast had finally come out of his trance or visions that he got from time to time.

Radagast was just in time, as Shichiro Lee took out his other sword, and in the native language that was used back then, they spoke and Shichiro Lee took out his other sword from off his shogun outfit that he had worn. It dripped of blood. Shichiro Lee looked as if his swipes with the sword could kill a lot easier than one might think. The killing of his six brothers over an argument and disrespect of honor, as well as his mother and father he had beheaded proved that point. Shiroicho stood for honor, and at such a young age never took disrespect from anyone, no matter who they were. It was a matter of pride and honor in all things. But something much larger would soon come. The shoguns were from the Imperial Clan, which was the largest clan in Japan, and that Shichiro was from. He looked at them, displaying his bruises and cut marks from knives and years of fighting.

He stood and said in his Japanese language that he would never fight in the honor of this clan ever again. Shichiro Lee wore armor with the faces of his mother and father on his chest and legs. He began to take it off, and the helmet that lay on the ground, he threw at one of the members of the team.

Now Shichiro stood in his underwear and his bare chest, revealing scars and red blood markings from the beating that he had taken over the years from his family members. As the others stood there ready for the revenge on Shichiro Lee, he stood, marked on his chest and back and arms and legs. There wasn't a part of him that hadn't been marked from a beating that he had taken. It was an awe-inspiring sight to behold.

He stood with the armor on the ground. Shichiro, the most vicious of them all, had the look of death on his face. His eyes did not belie any fear, as he had no fear and wasn't afraid of anyone or anything at all. Radagast and the emperor had picked up on this right away. It was something that was very easy to see.

Shichiro took his sword and, with his two hands holding it in a stabbing position, he destroyed the armor in ceremonial fashion, as the faces of his family had been destroyed. Shichiro took up the other sword that lay on the ground, and with the point of the sword, stabbed it and threw the helmet off the sword with such a strong motion that it smashed the face of one of the soldiers and killed him.

He had eleven opponents left. As they all charged him, he was quick and struck true, as he motioned his sword outward. Out of his sword came small ten-inch knives, which killed three more soldiers.

The soldiers, who had been previously fully charging, backed away a bit. But Shichiro stood firmly, as he had killed more than they thought he could without the help of the armor.

The warrior didn't wait but charged, as the others had fallen to the ground. He ran towards them with just something covering his privates, and no boots or anything on, just two swords in his hand.

The emperor, watching, was surprised and more impressed than he would like to admit.

Shichiro charged the others, and with his high-powered martial moves, in a matter of minutes he had destroyed a band of highly trained shoguns, cutting and beheading them, covering them in blood, and many other maneuvers not many fighters could perform.

As he stood over them, he turned back to look at the emperor and smile. There was something about him that Emperor Tashbi liked. There was a mighty gathering around, as some of the people had seen what this kid was capable of doing. Radagast had seen this already in his vision, and what he knew the history of what was to come. He tried to warn the others as well, but they chose not to listen to him in the vision that he had showed them.

The emperor walked over towards Shichiro and called his name. He had smiled as he looked at him. "Put down the swords, my son," he said. The swords were covered in blood from cutting the limbs of the warriors' arms and legs off, after being an untouchable warrior. That was without any protection on his body that he had managed this feat.

Shichiro looked hard at the emperor. He had ordered his own shoguns to dump the bodies and dispose of them, hiding them. He didn't care what they did with them at this point, as long as they were out of sight.

Radagast walked very slowly behind his emperor. He knew now that the groundwork had been laid to create The Dark Legend of The Foreigner. Of course, there were still many things to happen before he would even be born. Radagast had too many things to even think of at this point, but he knew that his fate and life were to always be connected to him in all ways possible. Radagast realized, taking in Shichiro, it was going to cause something much more significant than what the emperor could know.

His power continued to grow and his sense of destruction was more centered on that desire than anything else. He felt more and more power growing, as his army continued to expand in numbers and strength as well. The emperor had known it as well. The Imperial Clan had taken a major hit, thanks to Shichiro and the backlash from their youngest son as well. There was no fear from either one of them, as time had gone on from when Shichiro and the emperor had paired together. It was a match purely made from hell. Truly, they were the perfect match for one another.

Radgast had no say, and his word over the years had faded gradually over time. Radagast was not one to reason, as reasoning with someone who just wanted death was far beyond what his vision had shown him. Realizing that it was the fate of Japan and there was nothing he could ever do, he had no choice but to allow that moment to happen. That was probably the worst part about it, he thought. He couldn't do anything to stop the future from coming.

It was what Radagast had signed up for, and he realized the power he had, as well as what he would be doing in regard to making the decision that he had made. There were visions and a recurring dream that Radagast had about a very large black demon. It puzzled him, and he couldn't understand who the demon was or what its purpose was. For years and years after the first encounter with Shichiro, he never quite understood the connection the black demon had with this story at all. But, he knew it had a very powerful impact that was very meaningful. It was never part of what he was led to believe in his own personal journey with The Master, Shichiro's son-to-be.

Emperor Tashbi had exerted much of his time and effort from the day he had met Shichiro Lee. As part of building and enforcing a strong shogun clan, his fortunate discovery of Shichiro Lee was one of the greatest things that could have happened. He had finally found his clan leader, which he knew would be the case from the day that he had seen him do battle. Just as Emperor Tashbi had taken the time to train the warriors that were the protectors in his army, he now spent the time training Shichiro Lee. He was something special, as it had been a few years since he had discovered castle Alonga in Shizuoka. It was their home since the early 1600s. Emperor Tashbi had been very busy, building his army, creating a modern empire, and building an establishment that he could run and be extremely successful in Japan.

There was much more than just that, too. He truly had been looking for a destroyer in his army, someone who could lead it and conquer the other clan that would challenge his empire. His mission had taken years and years to accomplish. Japan and the surrounding villages and clans had noticed that Emperor Tashbi had built such an empire that it would be impossible to stop him. His army had been much too strong, having the strength of many shoguns put together. This all fell into place because of Shichiro Lee.

Shichiro Lee fulfilled his purpose: he had an imperial armor among one of the fiercest shoguns to ever walk the Japanese land. His reputation was just a vicious as his leader, and Radagast, along with the emperor, had seen what he had turned into. There was no sympathy in his heart. His swords were his closest friends, always in his hands. Radagast had spent all of his time with the emperor and had seen what type of fighter and Shichiro Lee had become. He knew that his son would become even worse that his father. There was no one who could truly stop him now. Shichiro Lee was grown up, and a fully developed young man. He was in his mid-twenties, and like the emperor's empire, he had some battles over the years and had become even more hardened due to his experience.

It was during the training in the beginning of the Shike war between all the clans that had built up fifteen years after the great tsunami, which had destroyed most of the clans and had killed many. Emperor Tashbi's greatest clan and empire was the youngest out of all the surrounding ones, near and far away. But his was the most powerful one, with all of the resources and money that the emperor had. His army was now in the hands of one of the most powerful warriors that would ever exist.

Radagast had seen from the start the rise and what would eventually be the fall of the emperor, but nothing came without a price. Everything had its cost in the end. The emperor's other generals had great contacts between the regions and would get information between their contacts. They were very careful to blend in and hide near other clans and get the information sometimes by killing other guards and dressing like other shogun warriors to keep from getting caught by the other clan members from other posts. It was the way that the emperor wanted things, as Shichiro Lee had kept up his army back at the post where he had trained all the warriors. It was his duty to do so. He had many men to train, and his body was built unlike most, from any decade for a Japanese man. It was very uncharacteristic for a woman to be in the army, but these men were worthless, as they couldn't fight or defend themselves, let alone protect any animal or, more importantly, the emperor. He had a certain woman in mind for the duty, Lin Shin. He had observed her and had a feeling that she could be a good addition to his army.

Shichiro Lee had called for open tryouts, as the men he had were worthless in the fight that was brewing and the war that was headed towards them swiftly. Shichiro Lee was focused on protecting the castle and the emperor. Radagast knew that this was all supposed to happen and saw how it was all falling into place. Radagast himself had finally grown a long beard, and he had grown old from his thoughts and his feelings towards everything. His skin, his hair, and his face all looked worn. The knowledge he had inside him had become a burden over the span of the last twenty-five years, and it had taken a toll on him.

He had seen all the things that he could have believed and not truly understood, but it was completely out of his power, and the way that power had always changed. He would destroy and alter a lot more than he would know as well. As times had changed, so did everything that he had believed and seen and told the others as well. When Shichiro had confronted the emperor about adding a woman to his military, the emperor had laughed at him, and told him he was crazy to do that.

He said, "That woman is weak and useless."

But he didn't press him too much. He knew by watching her from a distance that he was impressed, and he knew this war would not be won without her.

Radagast watched him leave the emperors' chambers, and Shichiro stormed out like he was angry about that one decision. His anger seemed to continue to grow, as he walked away from him in more ways than one.

He made his way to the combat area, which had been set up inside the castle grounds. The woman hadn't left after watching the training for what seemed like days. It was just that he had taken noticed, and Shichiro Lee wondered how long she had been watching. But to him, each day that he had come out from the chambers of the castle, it seemed she was still there from the night before.

It was as if she studied the way that they fought, but she was a fighter herself, and she had learned enough things over the years as well. She was a lot tougher than he thought she was. It was impossible to understand at this point. Shichiro Lee had completely disregarded anything that the emperor had said or warned him about. It was as if he had something even heavier on his mind. He had been anxious about him. He was a warrior himself, but Shichiro was something more than just that, and the emperor was a bit nervous about that as well.

That had scared the kingdom, as if Shichiro was the one who would lead the fight against the threats by the opposing ones against the others. Shichiro went and watched the others fight in his presence. He watched them all fall and get hurt. A great threat to the surrounding clans that thought the emperor's powerful army would take down the most powerful emperor that had taken years to build and spend most of their time trying to improve. Schichiro knew things would not go his way if he did not agree to his demands, and acquiesce to what he wanted.

However, Shichiro grew very impatient to his request, so ultimately, he went completely against what he had wanted. It wasn't as if the emperor would turn his back on Shichiro. That would not be wise. After all, no matter what kind of weapon he had in his weapon chamber, there was no weapon that could have been used to hurt him, nor was there one person who could effectively use them against him. He was a fighter, and a very good one at that.

The emperor had begun to be frightened by Shichiro as well, and even more so now, watching him completely go against what he had told him. He gave Lin Shin a sword and started training her. Because she had watched him for weeks and weeks, she learned quickly. She was good, and before long, she was as good as he was, if not better. How was a woman just as capable of doing what Shichiro was able to do? That was impossible to think that a woman was able to execute that kind of fighting ability. It was a testament to how she had trained from morning to night, poised and dedicated as she was.

Lin Shin was capable of much more than any of the soldiers that were already under Shichiro. Radagast had watched and knew at this point it was coming, and time had eased his pain. Truly, no one could understand what was to come, nor predict when it was coming. But it was something that was a long time brewing, as he could see the two warriors become what they were meant to be, after the months and months of training. Even the emperor had a hard time controlling the two monsters. There was nothing that the emperor could have done. He had lost complete control of them, and even trying to talk sense into them was futile. More so when the attempt to reason came from an emperor obsessed by power and destruction.

Over time, Lin Shin and Shichiro developed a close bond. They sensed an innate compatibility with one another, and their relationship grew stronger the longer they trained together. Each respected the other's abilities, and they found a certain common ground in their ideals and their single-minded sense of purpose to fight. They both were warriors at heart, and this drew them toward one another. No one else would have the same level of understanding that they each had for the other. As they grew closer and closer to one another, their relationship deepened into a romantic attachment.

The two lovers united in this way were a deadly combination. There was not one general that Emperor Tashbi could trust because they were afraid to cross the two feared warriors; as an empire once evoking fear by its emperor was now afraid of the new warriors in charge. That word began to spread quickly across the land. The two warriors, Lin Shin and Shichiro Lee, who were bound together, had created a deep fear of them, which was deeply instilled in everyone. There was nothing stopping them, as they knew that the emperor, who had taken Shichiro in, was now the one who feared for his life under their power.

The red wizard had warned him of this great fear years ago, but he had chosen not to listen. It was time, as Radagast had shown his loyalty to this point, but he knew what was coming. He couldn't do a damn thing about it, either.

He bowed, and said simply, "I have failed you," then disappeared into smoke, as the old and winded wizard vanished in an instant.

He made his way to Okla, where he would live out his remaining days . . . until he would have to defend against something even greater than the Lees.

The emperor was destroyed as the people had run for their lives. The Lees had made their bond official and had gotten married, but they had killed the person who married them because it had taken him too long to do it.

They both dressed like no warrior anyone had seen before. They only carried swords, and their armor was as strong as anything. They had completely destroyed the emperor's castle and the people that were left to kill and murder in cold blood. Things were left destroyed and people left dead: innocent people, men, women, and children. There was no one left breathing or with any hopes of getting away.

The Lees had formed such a powerful bond that there were no animals left alive either. They were deadly and frightening at the same time. The smell of dead bodies, and things destroyed from the hands of the Lees, permeated. It was a war that had been brewing all along, and the last clan that was left were the two warriors that remained, even with the ways that they had been outnumbered and feared from the start. It was inevitable.

Each of them had headed toward the destruction of the castle, and the smoke that had been evident. Fires were evidence that the empire had been destroyed, but not by other clans. It was finally time, as the emperor stood and came out from his headquarters, ready for a fight, and donning his two swords.

Lin Shin was hanging off the side of the stairs, and the emperor didn't see where she was. He heard the noise of her moving and saw her take a swipe with her sword, swiftly cutting the emperor in half. His body was cut, and blood was everywhere. There had already been blood shed of soldiers and innocent people alike, whose bodies were strewn amidst the layers of destruction and death. There was red all over, and things broken in half, nothing left and no one left alive. Even the emperor's body had been stuck in stone, as the blood of the Lees' names was written on what was left of the castle in the stone that it was made of.

#

Then, it was finally the end of the war, the Shike War, and finally they had come to the last and remaining castle. It was much greater than any of them could have expected, as each clan grew more and more powerful, building their strength in numbers. It was this clan that had over 100 men, women, and children, and not one person was living where the Lees were.

The destroyer clan had amassed soldiers from all of the other five clans, as over the years, it strategically moved from clan to clan and overtook each one in order to gain the power required to compete against the most powerful emperor. One of the many soldiers and shoguns had seen the complete destruction of Emperor Tashbi, and he thought, how hard would it be to take down two people? Little did they know, it would be a fight, as they had become the most feared two people in the land of Japan. The destroyer clan scattered all around from the green plants and woods that they took months and months to conquer, all the other clans and secret things having been done. It was hard to understand and imagine how good these two warriors were, and how deadly they had become, as word had traveled through the land that they had destroyed their own kingdom, and they were the most feared ones in the land for doing so.

The destroyer clan had so many shoguns that had traveled far and wide in order to come close to where Castle Shizuoka was. It was in ruins, thanks to the Lees.

The Lees stood and watched the destroyer clan come running out of the green forest. They were perched on top of the castle, what was left of it, anyway. They watched, and they both knew that the fighters were coming, and they really didn't expect a light battle, either. There was nothing that they hadn't anticipated, and they were prepared for anything.

The two warriors stood in a high-powered armor that hadn't been seen before on any other shoguns. It was like they had emerged from a different era, though clearly, they weren't. It was something that Shichiro Lee had been working on for some time. He had a blacksmith mold these black shogun outfits and had even thought about making a second, just in case. It was a one-size-fits-all pattern. The blacksmith had taken the time right before all the chaos had begun. The color of the shogun outfit was all black, and it was topped by a helmet that covered all except the eyes, with a separate opening for the warriors to breathe. The arms and legs were covered in spikes. Its metal was so strong that no sword could penetrate the metal. It was stronger than any sword that was used against the metal outfit as well. Most warriors would have a hard time damaging it, and there weren't many things that could combat it. It was also very easy to move with, as it wasn't too lightweight but not too heavy either.

The Lees had set their sights on the incoming destroyer clan, which they knew was about death and power, but so were the Lees. They were much more vicious than the most evil of the leaders. The Lees had visions of killing everyone in that clan, and they were quite capable of killing anyone and everyone that they could. With their armor and their abilities, so much better than anyone in the shogun army, the clan would be no match. It was hard to think that two people could destroy an entire army of shoguns, but in this case, the unimaginable was actually possible.

The Lees watched as the body count rise with all of their killings, and each of them smelled in a very foul manner. They had already known that this moment was coming. It was the impossible odds that had urged them on to fighter harder and harder for something that was so farfetched from ever happening. But, in their mind, it was not so out of reach. Impossible for most, yes, but not for them. They were the Lees and they had become the most feared fighters from clan to clan and throughout all of the land that would eventually become Japan. There wasn't one person who hadn't known about them, or their prowess, either. That's what made them scary. When an entire land talked about you, it was usually for good reason. Shichiro Lee they understood, but Lin Shin to have such a decisively solid reputation as well solidified their unified strength. It was as if nothing or no one would ever be capable of coming close to even slowing them down, let alone defeating them.

The Lees knew that this would be a fight to the death, and they also bore the knowledge that Lin Shin, a short Japanese woman, was carrying a baby, after only nine months of having met Shichiro Lee. They had formed a very strong bond and were inseparable at that point. There was something about how they had connected; it was mostly their passion for death and destruction. This was one of the primary things that had drawn them together more and more.

Shichiro was strong for such a little man, but very quick and agile with his hands and feet. His thrusts and strikes were so deadly, he could destroy anyone with his bare hands. The fierce warrior was only 5'8" and when given a sword, anyone in his path had better run for their lives. Lin Shin was a force to be reckoned with, too, just as deadly as he was. Neither one of them was too tall, but their strength and fast strikes more than made up for their slight frames.

Lin Shin's calves and leg strength were very powerful, and her ability to use a sword was remarkable. Shichiro Lee didn't have to train her much, as she knew a lot about swords and how to use them, and her fighting ability was solid. She had much more intuitive skills and capabilities than he thought she would have. But, a lot of people tended to judge before they saw what a person had. Lin Shin was only 5'5" and for a small woman of her frame, she had a solid build.

She was more than most of the destroyer's clan. As most of them weren't too formidable in strength, Lin Shin was.

It was time to *shut up or die*, as the Lees had started their own little saying.

#

Meanwhile, Radagast was in his hideout in Okla. He knew what was going on, and what was headed in that direction. There was nothing the old white long-bearded wizard would do to alter any of the events to change the history of things. He was powerless to choose to do so either way, and he couldn't compromise the future, as it was meant to unfold.

Radagast had disappeared into the land of Okla, and that was where his remaining days would loom. A very gloomy and dark place it was among many things. Dark, cold, and a sense of death and a void of something was palpable there. Whether it be death or souls crying for something was uncertain. There wasn't much that could change the way Radagst thought. Maybe it was that he knew with the Shike War, it was so little time, but yet still far away from everything finally coming full circle.

For Radagast, he would have rather been banished to the Temple of Time where all the other wizards had gone after their own deaths. It was a fate of the darkest days that were coming for him. He would be the center of everything once again. Even though he was the youngest of all the other wizards, and the most powerful, altering time was one thing he could not do, nor change the course of history. If one thing changed, it would set off a domino effect, and things would become out of balance. He knew the war was starting and that was something he needed to avoid being around.

The Lees watched from the top of the destroyed castle from very far away. They spoke to each other in such an ancient language that not even the destroyer clan could understand or grasp their meaning. It was a language that had been forgotten in the land's history, and only a select few had known it. In just another commonality that drew them together, it just so happened that both Lees were raised being taught that language. It was a forgotten language, as it was one of the most difficult to understand and use. Even in the 1600s, it had been isolated as an uncommon one, while a more common one was being used, to make it much simpler. Most of the destroyer clans used the common language that was used in Japan today.

The destroyers continued to pour out of the woods and the army of shoguns came running toward the others, as each group moved closer and closer to the castle. The dead bodies that had covered the dirt had quickly been trampled over and destroyed by the heavy footwear of the destroyer clan. They were adorned with symbols of family markings on their legs, and their helmets told what type of clan they represented as well.

The two Lees had watched the fray, as the loud footsteps echoed, and the footsteps vibrated the earth, more and more vicious with every footstep that advanced, shaking the ground beneath their feet. Upon hearing the approach, the Lees hadn't moved a muscle after what they had felt. They remained motionless.

As for the looks on both their faces, they remained stoic, their expressions impossible to discern. Were they scared as hell? Or fearless, as was their typical nature? It was difficult to discern by looking at them, and their eyes hadn't blinked at all for anything. Even as the clouds opened up, and the fire burned throughout the castle, eventually, the fires would be put out, but the damage that the Lees had done had crossed to a point of no return.

As the heavy footsteps closed in, the Less had finally moved, and they came down the broken castle steps. In the wind, the ripped flag swayed, a reminder of the marked territory of Emperor Tashbi's former castle. There was no fear, not in anything they encountered, nor fate. For their part, the Lees knew that they wouldn't face it. One may call it confident or hubris, but they truly weren't afraid of anyone or anything. There was not one thing that had entered their hearts that had made them face fear. They believed the smell of fear was a sign of weakness. That was a trait that neither one of them had ever shown to the other.

The Lees continued down what was left of the stairs of the castle. Their eyes were as intense as ever, and their countenances had darkness written all over them. The blackness of the cold weather was palpable, and it wasn't just from the dampness of the cold rain that poured through the night. It was a perfect scenario for the Lees, as there wasn't much light remaining in the kingdom, or light from the sky. Under cover of dusk, there was created a fiery atmosphere for the events that were transpiring.

The Lees reached the bottom of the stairs, and a few of the destroyer leaders tried to have a conversation in a few words with them. Both sets of languages were not easy to translate back and forth.

The destroyer clan got little dialogue with them, and it was lucky that they even had the little bit that they did. A few members talked, while Lin Shin or Shichiro Lee answered.

The heavy armor looked intimidating with its weight. It was as if the ten different clan members that had taken over the other clans to obtain power now thought that same power resided resoundingly with the Lees.

After a brief exchange, they finally agreed to meet. The ten members of the clan members would fight the two Lees. How would this end up? The outcome was uncertain. This didn't look like an easily commanded situation for the pair, being completely outnumbered by nine clans, and all the strength in numbers, too. It seemed the odds were against them, and the bodies were all lined up, the shoguns ready to do battle if the ten destroyer clan leaders all perished fighting the Lees. They had a massive amount of bodies to take out the Lees if all others would fail. At this point, who knew what was going to happen? It could be anyone's fight.

The Lees came down the final steps of the castle. They had a look of unwavering determination on both of them. One might expect their confidence to be shaken or fear to have infiltrated their minds, but nothing had changed. There was no honor that the Lees had for anyone or anything. They were vicious and heartless, ruthless warriors who had loyalty only to one another, and even that was tenuous. At heart, they were warriors before lovers. There had been so many things that were changing within the landscape of their homeland of Japan. The war, finally, was here. The Shike

War, which Radagast had warned all the others about, had come. Though Radagast knew the course of events that was to happen, not one of them had believed him.

Both Lin Shin and Shichiro had seen the fear in the faces of the clan leaders, each of the nine clan members that had formed the destroyer clan. Each face looked the same, as if all of them were about to piss in their armor. Each member had a different marking, showing the clan that they represented. There was one marking even greater than that, which they all had—the mark of fear. Whether it was the shogun leaders from the separate clans or the other ones who would die protecting the land, fear was their common ground. Though not one of them would admit it, it was fear of the Lees that overpowered them all. The Lees had clearly sensed this as well. Like a wolf on the hunt, the Lees smelled blood, the blood and heart of the souls that they were ready to kill. No one would be able to stop them.

If the leader of the shoguns from the different clans could sense the same, how in the world would the others, there to help kill the Lees, overcome this? The Lees were on the ground, and the armor was very frightening for the common shogun.

Meanwhile, Radagast sat in his little hut in Okla with the precognition that a blood bath was about to happen. He saw what most couldn't or wouldn't either. There was so much that he had seen: utter chaos, turmoil, and death. But it wasn't to be at any point. Radagast sat in his home and was kneeling on a pillow, reciting a special prayer, while he looked at the pictures that were hung up on the wall in his house.

Radagast, filled with disgust and rage, stood up, his face contorting. The more he thought, the angrier he got. Before he could stop himself, he began to destroy things, pulling pictures off the wall, and knocking over furniture and objects that were directly in front of him. At this point, Radagast was at a loss as to how to process his feelings or react to the things he knew. The burden had become too much to bear.

The Lees stood on the ground of Tashbi's temple, now half destroyed. Lin Shin and Shichiro were surrounded by many different clan members who had found themselves confronting an unstoppable force.

The Lees faced several types of adversity in that moment. Coming to light was their union, which they had both been hiding, as it was forbidden back then. Their relationship had remained in secret. While Shichiro had trained Lin Shin to be the fighter, which she had always had in her, her anger and frustration over the years had transformed her into a much deadlier weapon that most could ever imagine. The fact that she was expecting was another thing entirely that would have to be reckoned with. They both knew this was a way out, but it had come much sooner than either one of them had anticipated. These were some heavy shoes that had to be worn at this point.

The fact remained evident that they had destroyed what was left of Tashbi's castle, and other clans came from hundreds and hundreds of miles to kill him, and his army. There wasn't much left of the army, as most of the bodies had been slaughtered and left all over the territory of the castle and the land before it as well. The Lees had wiped out Emperor Tashbi's army, which Shichiro had trained. He was one deadly weapon by himself. There was nothing nor no one that could compete with him. His training of Lin Shin secretly behind the Emperor's back merely enhanced his own power.

They both stood down not far from the sounds of the forest. The slightest pin drop could be heard. An unsettled current in the air settled like fog, as the crickets and the sounds of the night began to creep in. Some of the different clan members knew of Shichiro and his reputation. However, they hadn't known anything about the woman; who or what she was remained a mystery. This served as a secret weapon of sorts.

The comments in the native language had rarely been used, and the old way was fading out to a new phase. It wasn't the Lee's way, though. The other clan had begun using the new form, while the Lees had used a language that was from the old way of speaking. They all understood their tongue, though.

Shichiro stood down and all ten other members had surrounded them. The Lees had their backs to each other, and words flew back and forth between the Lees and the others that now seemed like an army to stop two warriors. No one had ever seen Lin Shin fight, and it was going to be something beyond all of their imaginations.

Shichiro's body language spoken an even greater common language to them all as he emoted severe anger. When it came to the Lees, they could bicker all they wanted, but reasoning of any sort was out of the question.

Just then, Lin Shin drew her sword. Her sword was special, as it had the power of a boomerang. She quickly hurled it, bending it swiftly through the air. She moved quickly towards the ten clan members while her weapon cut through the air. They had no idea what to expect and could not have prepared for what was to come.

It had killed all ten with one throw from Lin Shin. As the heads of some were cut in half, others were left without arms and other body parts. There was immediate carnage wrought by her boomerang sword. The ten clan members were struck dead before even one could retaliate or draw his own weapon. The execution was definitive and exact, ensuring victory for the Lees with one decisive motion from Lin Shin, with Shichiro at her side. The sword returned itself to her, and she stood with shoulders square.

It was the beginning of the Shinnshe War.

It was a war that would last only five days. The Lees had battled for many miles, dismantling armies and bodies of many shoguns and killing hundreds and hundreds more. They felt no guilt about how they killed and why they pursued their course so relentlessly. The Lees were protecting their unborn child, and that was their main focus. There was nothing that anyone could do about it. They did what they wanted, and kill whomever they chose, and however they wanted. There was nothing that they couldn't do. They were supremely superior to all of them.

There was no one who could have stopped them, even all of their forces combined still falling short of the insurmountable task of defeating the Lees. It served to illustrate how vicious and unfalteringly cruel they were. The Lees had no regard for any human life besides their own and their unborn child, and they showed it through their actions.

As the Lees had an army of men, they stood on the backs of those who had been destroyed by them. They used their bodies to jump and fly through the air, in order to kill as many as they could. Their armor that they had worn protected every inch of their body from any sharp objects that might have killed or maimed them.

While so many of the shogun warriors had approached and taken their swipes at each of the Lees, the result was predominantly the same. There hadn't been much luck on their side. Many of the weapons that they had used had broken after attempting to use it on the Lees' armor. The ground was littered with countless broken swords and other weapons. What made it even more difficult was that hand-to-hand combat wasn't an option either, as the pair was truly impossible to defeat at the other end of the fight. These circumstances made it an extremely arduous task to defeat them. Even though they had been purely outnumbered by many, the sheer number was not enough to conquer them, and the level of combat they had acquired allowed them to win easily.

The sight and smell of the rotting dead bodies from the multitude of kills they had overpowered all who encountered it. Human guts fell out of men's bodies. The stench was incredible, and it was a sight that would overwhelm the senses and cause most to throw up immediately.

The castle was a different story entirely. On a magnified level, the destruction and ruination permeated the area. While the men dropped, the Lees were covered from head to toe, and there was nothing short of victory as a two-week battle stemmed from the beach side to where the castle was, then to a very wooded area. It was one way that the Lees were able to kill so many. Their speed and agility were no match.

Many times, they were chased down between areas, and other times fell into traps that they had set, in order to kill shoguns in abundance. It was the way that they had outsmarted and outmaneuvered their foes. Traps that had been in place from Emperor Tashbi's kingdom found new purposes. They had used devices, which were still in working order. They were many—the poison darts, the drop pits, and the shogun army room that came to life. There were all sorts of rooms and traps in the castle. It was unsettling and disturbing to behold. With heads put through spikes, as if once you walked into the castle you wouldn't be walking out alive, the stage was set for further violence. It was an easy assumption and an inevitable one at that.

There were pictures on the wall that depicted death and various ways of dying. The castle was truly fraught with death and dying. Even when the Lees had escaped a few times, the very scattered occurrences, the outcome was still the same. Outsmarting the shoguns was typical in the war. There hadn't been many who had used their brains. That was what they had wanted, but the Lees were too smart and had keen insight when it came to war.

As shogun group after shogun group was killed, by the entrance of the castle, by their swift swordsmanship, or by numerous other ways, the scales were tipped in favor of the Lees.

It had only taken the Lees two weeks to kill an army of shoguns; that would wipe out around 300 shoguns. The battle was gruesome and deadly, and the body count was higher than most could have imagined.

The Lees had conquered many shogun clans. The winds began to change, and the Lees stood victorious, as both of their swords were covered in blood, as were their bodies from head to toe. The only thing peeking out from the layers of gore were their eyes.

When the Lees looked around and saw what they had done, they smiled at the realization of how vicious and evil they truly were. They knew word would travel fast throughout the land that the Lees had conquered ten different shogun clans, as well as having killed each of their founding leaders and members. It was a devasting blow to the clans and the shoguns, especially considering that what transpired was in complete opposition to how things normally would progress in a war they should have easily won. It was clear that they weren't any normal shoguns or people.

They knew it would be only a matter of time before they would soon find another number of shoguns head their way. However, it would still take days to get to them. The Lees had time to figure out what to do and plot their next move carefully. They had to regain their bearings, while the darkness in the clouds intensified. It was something that the Lees had both noticed. It grasped their attention, and both of them looked, as the dark clouds completely immersed the land from all sides and angles.

It was as if an evil force advanced, and a new power of some sort that had been wanting to break out from a curse of a thousand years or more. There was something about the laugh that even caused the Lees to look a little afraid from the sight before them and that menacing laugh. It was something that made them both feel trepidation.

While this was going on, Radagast sat in his part of his house in Okla, having heard the ominous laughter as well. He knew exactly who it was. It was Orthor, a very powerful and dark warrior who had been vanquished and defeated 5,000 years ago. Radagast knew that this wasn't a good sign and an omen of things yet to come. Many of his other wizard friends had dealt and fought against him, never to break a curse that was placed on him. Radagast knew that things were now out of his control, and he never thought this would happen in his lifetime, as he was supposed to have been killed and not left alive in a universe that not even the great Radagast could have ever reached.

Radagast had a very bad feeling about this, his fear mounting with the fact that he knew the story of the Lees and how they came to be. But it was the fact that he knew that Lin Shin had been carrying a child, a product of both of them. He knew somehow that his fear extended outside himself to the rest of the world. Certainly, the Lees had left a mark on history, beyond all known bounds.

Meanwhile, the Lees had gathered all necessary provisions, including warm clothes, and they formulated a plan to head up to the mountains in Okla. They needed as much as they could carry in preparation to flee the area of where they were. They had no horses and no readily accessible way of getting up that steep mountain, except by foot, one step at a time. It was a huge mountain, and for them to get up there from where they were would be an arduous journey.

Shichiro and Lin Shin had gathered their weapons and whatever else they could grab for protection and survival— whatever they could carry on their back without becoming too burdened by the climb. It was something that they needed to do. But what made them wonder was that creeping darkness and evil that had blanketed the land. It was something so out of the blue unnatural that it nearly gave them pause, before they steeled themselves and embarked on a long journey up the mountain.

#

Back at Okla, Radagast had been doing whatever he could do to find information in the books that he had. His little hut was a mess and books and other things were strewn all over the floor from his outburst. It was something that he had heard others talk about—who Orthor was. But, he never really asked probing questions, as it was something that none of the other wizards seemed comfortable discussing. It had a lasting effect on them and for all people for thousands and thousands of years after. Radagast knew never to ask questions about that matter.

Radagast was on his knees searching for one of the books that he had torn apart in his fit of rage. He looked around and sat Indian style on the floor in his red cloak. He opened the book he'd been looking for, and halfway through the old book, he found a passage that barely had anything on Orthor except his name and where he was from. It was impossible to get anything extensive about him, it seemed.

Radagast put the book containing the scarce research down alongside him. Orthor, he considered, was a conundrum. There was nothing on this warrior compared to the information provided for so many others in this one book. He was perplexed and didn't understand why there wasn't anything in any one of the books that he had and that were passed on to him by the other wizards from the Temple of Time.

He really hadn't any idea on how to proceed, and nor should he have, as Orthor was well before his time and he was the evilest of evil. Not even the devil could contend with his power or stop him. He was an eight-foot demon, very tall, muscular, an imposing figure, and the sight of him was horrifying to say the least.

Radagast had one last-ditch effort. He took a deep breath, sat and closed his eyes, and transported himself to the Temple of Time, where his body and soul had gone. As he stood and opened the solid metal door, he walked in as all the clouds had covered most of what was in front of him. It was like the other wizards were trying to prevent the most powerful one from seeing what should never have been seen. As humans, you always know when someone is hoping to conceal things. Radagast saw the same.

As Radagast spoke to the temple, he knew the others listened and that they didn't ever have to respond. He looked around in an area covered by clouds and mist that prevented him from seeing more than two feet in front of him. For Radagast to be in this position, the fate of the world was in jeopardy. It wasn't something that would affect the world today, but it was an eventuality that would have to be contended with in the future.

Finally, without a sound, images appeared and revealed Orthor 5,000 years ago, and the destruction and the death that he had brought, killing many, and his followers of demons and his dark horses, who led to conquer thousands and thousands of people—people who were killed because of Orthor and his powerful army. There was massive destruction that they had done between what was Europe and Asia.

It was a devasting effect and would take centuries to rebuild the land that was left in shambles. Radagast had seen everything—the devastation that plagued the land and what was left. How the wizards had worked together to put a curse that would only last 5,000 years, and how they couldn't kill him. They didn't have enough power and strength combined in order to kill such a powerful demon.

At some point in that amount of time, the Temple of Time was formed to have a place to go and, if needed, the help of others to take down the powerful Orthor or anyone else that would challenge the peace of the world. It was something that had to be done and so it was from that time on. It was a scary time that had passed and that still haunted them.

Orthor was a beast, and Radagast had gone back after learning of his power and about how his curse wasn't fully gone, but rather simply a few hundred years from wearing off.

When Radagast arrived back in Okla, he realized something was different. As he looked up at the stars, the timing of everything seemed off. He knew that it was way off, in fact, disrupted somehow, and he felt off balance.

The wizard fell to his knees and screamed a scream that echoed through the land of Okla. He knew what time it was. He had sent out birds to find the nearest shoguns alive, beseeching them to find them. The birds had taken weeks for a response and as they did, they approached him and the hut that was in the middle of nowhere. It had an air of mystery and suspicion for someone not knowing exactly what they would be walking into.

Radagast was called upon, as Rifica had got the messages from a good distance away, from the town of Okla.

Rifica called out, "Radagast!"

Behind him stood twenty shoguns. Rifica wore his helmet and held his sword by his side, as he continued to call out for Radagast to be summoned from his abode.

Slowly, the old wizard emerged from the hut. He walked with a cane in hand, and his old wrinkled skin revealed the passage of time much more so than his years would portray him to be.

As he regarded him, Rifica, the tribal leader, knew that indeed, it was Radagast.

"Come in," said Radagast, gesturing to his hut. The hut wasn't very large. It really couldn't fit more than a few people.

Rifica ducked his head and stepped over the many books that were lying on the floor. Radagast sat down, and the tribal leader followed suit.

He looked at him, and Radagast's face teemed with anger and disgust. It was a long and weary road that he couldn't understand where to begin, or how to start explaining. Okla was in the opposite direction from where the Lees had done their damage.

Eventually, Radagast began to tell Rifica everything that had happened, events leading up to the domination by the Lees: what they had done, the damage they had wrought, and the amount of men they had killed, along with assassinating ten clans of shoguns, who proved to be no match for them.

When Rifica learned of this, he was angered to the point of no return, his face strained with the vexation.

"I will make Okla my home for as long as possible," he said, looking at Radagast. Then, he got on his knees and bowed. "I shall avenge all of the families who have been mercilessly killed and destroyed," he vowed.

Radagast gave a weak smile as he looked at him. "The Lees are a very dangerous family, and a deadly one at that. There is no one who can truthfully stop them."

Somberly, Rifica nodded his assurance that he would seek revenge nonetheless. He stood and turned to leave the hut, determination in his eyes.

The tribal leader had ordered the shoguns to build their homes here. So, over a matter of months and years, that they did. Radagast knew that they were gone.

He informed Rifica that it was too late. The very dark Okla, especially near the mountain entrance, gave the appearance of having been cursed before even approaching the small and wooden path. It was an extremely shrubby area. But it had left an image that induced fear in most. It was miles and miles from where Radagast's home was and far enough to not think about because of its seclusion. It was a trip that would inevitably be taken to show Rifica what he had to know about everything that had transpired. Over many months, his crew and the families of some had been moved. Still, Rifica was a young man with the heart and desire to fight this predicament that Radagast was so obsessed with: somehow overcoming the Lees.

Radagast's time in the Temple of Time was something that he had not counted on doing himself. He had let the time go, and in that time, he had inadvertently let the Lees go up the mountain.

The Lees had traveled up the very co'' mountain, and they knew the survival rate would be sl.... However, as they were both fueled by the desire to defeat the odds, they were confident and believed that they both had a very special place in the history books, though not in a favorably depicted way.

The Lees had gone up into the mountain, an eventuality that Radagast had believed had happened based on the time that he had been detained in the Temple of Time. He knew there was nothing he could have done to alter any of the timing or sequence of events that happened either. It was a foregone conclusion that those things had happened as predicted. It was simply the time that it had to happen. For Radagast, there was nothing that would ever change it, nor could there have been.

With the thoughts of The Master and Orthor both looming, the stress had made Radagast age rapidly and prematurely. Radagast had known much more than he was letting on to Rifica. He had never told him, for instance, about the unborn son of the Lees. That was a whole other sense of impending danger that grew within Radagast. He had so much on his mind, but it was the one thing that had most affected him in a myriad of ways.

Radagast knew that there was a lot going on, and he had limited the amount of information for the time being that he told Rifica. It wasn't as if he would ever know that he was withholding information. That was something that Radagast alone knew, along with the fact that something much deadlier loomed in the future, perhaps something that the world would have never known to be.

It was a very different experience as Radagast and Rifica finally made the trip that had been talked about. Rifica had construction going on many things and made it function as a military lookout more than anything. He felt the energy that Radagast had put into his descriptions of everything that had happened as well. He had felt the things that he had described, and as Rifica followed in the footsteps, in his honor, he did his best to lead his men and shoguns in order to have them follow in a similar manner.

Radagast and Rifica both stood and stared at the front of the entrance to Okla mountain. Radagast had told Rifica what he wanted, and they both had plotted at length regarding what they thought would be the best way to defeat the Lees. Something they had both neglected to think of was the constant coldness of the mountain, where survival would be next to impossible. Rifica wasn't sending innocent men to their death before absolutely necessary. It was a death wish. Rifica agreed to patrol the entrance to the mountain for as long as it took. These were words that would come back to haunt him, eventually.

#

It was always dark around the entrance of the mountain, no matter what weather was happening closer to where Radagast and the other shoguns had been. An air of unease and creeping dread lurked around them in the permanent darkness, a void that consumed any happiness or joy, a true point of no return. Was it caused by an evil spirt or just fear of the Lees? So many questions were brought to mind when they thought about their impending battle with the pair of warriors. They paused, wondering.

But it made them truly consider the things that Radagast had already known. As they both stood at the entrance to the tall mountain and looked up, then down, they hesitated. They both stood at the entrance, wondering about the Lees and their fate.

Radagast knew so much of everything, but Rifica was in the dark about some things. But there were many questions about things both known and unknown. Even Radagast had not known when, or who, Orthor was, and he had no idea what his connection to the Lees would be. There were so many lingering questions that would need to be answered at some point.

Radagast looked as Rifica began to walk away. He often found himself with this inner turmoil, wondering about what he knew and when certain events would happen. It was a curse that left knots in Radagast's stomach. It was the uncertain timing of everything that gnawed at him most— the questions he couldn't answer and the things he couldn't prepare for. It was simply human nature. That is what made him the way he was, with a need for planning. It was the stark fact that he couldn't plan or prepare for anyone or anything that would keep him up at night. When would these things come to pass and release him from this constant worry?

At least in terms of the child, he knew he had many years to prepare for him. Orthor, on the other hand . . . he really had no idea if or when he would ever come into to play, or if he even would appear. But the fact remained that he still had years before that curse would finally end.

Radagast stood there, pondering. The darkness of the entrance to Okla began to cover what light had been covered by the mountain, and before long, it covered the entire town of Okla and its entrance. It was an all-consuming, complete darkness that was only the beginning. As Rifica looked back at Radagast standing by the entrance of Okla, he turned to see if Radagast had moved. But the wizard had not, though being in complete darkness made it difficult to see even from a short distance away. The time when the world would be changing fast approached, and Radagast knew that no matter why this was happening, the darkness was coming.

Chapter 3

*A*s The Lees approached Okla mountain, they stood looking at the entrance to the imposing summit. Over the years they had heard numerous stories of the Okla mountain being haunted. There was no one who truly wanted to even go near that mountain. The fact that they had been standing in front of it was a success in its own right, considering most hadn't wanted to even go near the entrance to the mountain.

It had been a journey by foot, lugging heavy furs and anything that would give them warmth. As Okla mountain was a very cold mountain, it never experienced any fluctuations in temperature or weather. Still breathing after traveling a few days, the Lees owed this to the multitude of items they needed to survive. It was that or take the chance of always being on the run from the shoguns, who would eventually kill them. Instead of 300, they would send more, as word had traveled throughout the land about what the Lees had done.

They knew that their only choice was to flee, and that had been the only option for any chance of survival. Even facing the bitter cold, as cold as could be imaginable, there was truly no other option but that. They had left their armor and most of their weapons that would weigh them down. They were survivors who knew how to do that.

Both of the Lees had been through very rough childhoods that they were both able to overcome and survive. It had made them mentally tough. Still, yet another obstacle they had to deal with was Lin Shin's pregnancy, as there were no doctors whose aid they could seek in the 16th century. Especially being in Japan, a far cry from the rest of civilization.

They both had their wools, while their body armors were left behind, as they weren't anything that they needed in order to survive. The weather was their most treacherous enemy at this point and if anything would be the one thing that would kill them, it was the natural elements. They needed to survive, and surviving against the mountain and its fierce temperature and winds would be the one thing they needed to do to carry on.

They continued to regard the eerie entrance to Okla mountain. It was evident from their facial expressions as they looked at one other that they sensed the same feeling of unease and trepidation. Very fierce warriors, they had been left with little choice but to have killed the shoguns in the epic blood bath. This culmination was the result of their deeds, and they now knew that they would not have chosen to constantly be on the run from all the shoguns, who would not stop looking for them until they were killed. It was a fairly easy decision to make.

Lin Shin being pregnant was assurance that, at least, they would have their baby live on and carry on their name, despite not having the technology to be able to tell what sex the baby was. There were so many things that they could only imagine and wish for. But in their hearts, they hoped their child would be a boy.

The Lees stood in front of the mountain, their sacks on the ground, mostly filled with things that would keep them warm, and a few swords— mostly their weapons of choice—so that they would not be totally defenseless. It was scary, cold, and dark, just like all the stories that were told to them as children. It was something that had stuck with them as kids and was not coming to life in their adulthood. But the stories they remembered about the things within this mountain were never proven to be false either. Now here they stood in front of the extremely dark and cold entrance, which would make anyone near it shiver, even with the proper warm clothes to combat the frigid air.

They had no other choice and knew with certainty what needed to be done. Their faces belied their resolution, though, as they regarded the task in front of them with a hint of dread. The climb would be arduous, as they would need to traverse the snowy mountain with no horses or any other animal. Even if they did have a companion, most animals would have run away upon seeing the entrance to the mountain.

The whistling of the mountain, the wind, the cold, and the fact that this mountain hadn't seen any light as long as anyone could have remembered brought forth a terrifying feeling. As they speculated about what might befall them, for better or worse, they knew it was time.

Lin Shin looked around as they headed into the forest where the ground was thickest with snow. She retrieved a few large walking sticks not too far from the entrance to the mountain.

"Here," she said, handing one to Shichiro Lee.

"Thank you," he said simply.

Lin Shin's resourcefulness had made her think to use it as a walking stick in order to have some sort of balance. This would prove to be one of the smartest moves at this juncture, since the snow that blanketed the ground would otherwise make for unsure footing along the way. They also didn't know what other conditions they might encounter on the mountain either. It was good planning. They both picked up, heaved a shared sigh between them, and started up the mountain.

"We can make it," Shichiro assured his warrior partner and wife.

"We must," Lin Shin agreed. "We have no other choice."

Neither one of them knew that shoguns were in pursuit, and they would soon have to face an even greater challenge than they'd imagined.

The Lees headed up the mountain, their sacks on their backs, and both their swords, graced by their black and red shogun colors that they both wore proudly. It wasn't something that they had ever neglected to wear. As they climbed, they were keenly aware of the armor that they had left behind, realizing how much it would have weighed them down. The steep mountain, with its hilly parts and rough terrain, would leave anyone breathless from just looking up at the peak, never mind attempting to make the journey to reach it.

They had a long journey ahead, and they had wool wrapped around most of their bodies. The intense winds were gusting heavily, and the walking sticking that both of them were of great use while they battled the intense wind and cold. Every step was a challenge. They had a long distance left to go. It was a struggle to move, as along with the wind and cold, everything was covered in blinding white snow, so neither of them could easily see where they were walking. Okla mountain was like this most of the year, so it wasn't anything that the mountain hadn't seen before. Still, the mountain never had anyone crazy enough to experience firsthand the dangerous and brutal conditions. No one, at least, had ever survived to tell about it.

Okla was ten times worse than Mount Everest would be, and even more dangerous. They had journeyed for a few days, and their food was mostly cold and frozen, making it too difficult to eat. They both had a lot of resilience to make it up the mountain and had used every ounce of energy to push through the unrelenting conditions.

It was hard for the Lees to see in front of them as well. This merely added another layer of danger to the already treacherous surroundings. The Lees had nothing to protect their eyes, and the white of the snow, combined with the wind was grueling. Eyes being most precious commodities and irreplaceable ones at that, the Lees were in peril of being severely hindered.

After a three-day battle, using every ounce of energy and breath to finally get to a resting place in the midst of a heavy storm, they were both cold and shivering. Their mental toughness waned in light of the near-fatal conditions. The atmosphere endangered them, and they were both weak lack of water or sustenance. It was scary and dangerous to an extreme degree. Their eyes were hurting, there were sweating, dehydrated, and weak with hunger and fatigue. It was more than most would have ever survived.

Ironically, as Lin Shin grabbed Shichiro's hand, it was evident that he was the weaker one, despite that she was the one who was pregnant. All the while, she battled contractions, along with the fierce conditions of the mountain. She signaled suddenly. She saw a house that seemingly had smoke coming from a small hut that looked extremely secure and sturdy.

Each step seemed like they were inching closer to their last. Lin Shin approached the door and saw the handle was frozen shut. Shichiro Lee and Lin Shin both tried smashing themselves against the door to try to open it. After a few attempts, they were able to make it happen. On the last attempt, they were able to get the door open, in spite of the heavy wind. They pushed the door all the way open and entered the hut. Inside, they felt the warmth and stability of the structure.

Upon entering, it seemed as though someone had the house completely set up to be inhabited by one or more people. There was wool placed all over the hut for warmth. It made things simple, as they were walking into a good situation, especially since all the layers that they had on weren't nearly enough. Now they could put on extra layers that had been left on the chairs and scattered all around.

The sturdiness of the house was able to support the brutal strength of whatever winter storm might come this way. They also found a wooden fireplace, where soon they made a strong fire burning, and the windows had been protected and boarded up from the inside. It was a smart way of being protected from the conditions up in the mountains.

There were many things that just fell into place in a good stroke of luck. They sat by the fire, removed the cold fur, and put on the wool that had not been used. It had been days that their bodies were freezing, and they were still shaking. Sitting with gloves still on, the water that dripped off the wool from the snow pooled at their feet. They both felt lucky to be alive.

Lin Shin was hunched over. Her stomach and back hurt with the labor pains of her pregnancy, and she did not know the timing of everything. They had only averaged it from what they remembered, but it wasn't as if doctors could tell them what to expect or when. They were both on high alert, and Shichiro tried to help, but his body was worse than hers was from their arduous journey up the mountain, and from years of being a fierce warrior, longer than she had been.

They had both been battling the unimaginable cold. Shichiro Lee suddenly fell to the ground and his eyes rolled into the back of his head.

Lin Shin, despite being in labor, tried to drag his body as close to the fire as possible, without being burned.

She lay flat on the floor and knew right away that something was wrong through sheer instinct—it wasn't as if she had a mother around to tell her what to expect. With Shichiro lying on the ground, freezing and unconscious, it left her with little option. She was on her own with no one to help her.

Lin Shin's pants were off now, in preparation for the baby, and the circulation in her body was limited. Her baby's father was lying on the ground, motionless. They truly didn't know what was going on. It felt as if something was coming out of her vagina, but beyond that, nothing could assist her with the procedure she'd need to endure next.

She was pushing and pushing, a painful expression on her face, while she called out Shichiro's name and tried to remain composed and in control at the same time. Yes, he still lay there, out like a light, for what seemed like an endless amount of time. Lin Shin managed to remove her underwear, while she writhed in pain, arching her back. Her voice could have woken the dead with the screams she emitted.

Shichiro Lee lay there, still, not offering any assistance or even showing signs of waking soon.

The labor had lasted about an hour so far, a long time of sweating and yelling and pushing—a very grueling labor. It wasn't easy for her by herself as Shichiro lay inert on his back, and she had no idea if he were dead or alive. However, she could only worry about herself and her soon-to-be-born baby at that time. Both were lucky to be alive as well.

A fleeting thought told her they hadn't any idea what part of the mountain that they were on or any direction. But that was not the concern at the moment. Lin Shin had one concern, and that was to stop the pain from occurring. She hadn't understood how the pregnancy would progress and affect her in the moment, and she was now realizing what was truly going on.

Finally, after about 45 minutes of intense pushing and screaming, the ordeal was finally over, and she completed her birthing of a newborn child.

The sound of a baby crying in the middle of the hut finally roused Shichiro, and he gave a slight movement of his head. He began to show signs of life, and the baby's screams seemed to bring him back into the waking world, with the knowledge that both he and Lin Shin were still alive, along with a new addition to their family.

It was so cold, windy, and snowy up in Okla mountain on that night, as Lin Shin began to nurse their new baby. There hadn't been too many other signs of life. It was for good reason no one would be stupid enough to enter those mountains and go up in those conditions, the way Radagast had wanted.

Takeo, the shogun who had agreed to help Radgast, knew that Okla mountain was far too cold, and they both knew that it was simply a matter of waiting, and nothing more than that.

#

In the early years, Lin Shin and Shichiro focused on the growth of their son, whom they dubbed "The Master." He wasn't like anything that they could imagine. Both proud parents saw signs of strength and near-expert technique even when the child was just a few months old. It led them both to believe that he was going to be something much greater than they could have predicted, more powerful than both of their warrior skills combined, even. At least, they acknowledged, the potential was there. Time would tell if their child would surpass his parents in skill and power. Meanwhile, all three adapted to the tough living conditions and the cold of the unforgiving mountain. They did what they had to in order to survive.

The living conditions were cold, and the days were long. During those hard months made, they seemed to face more challenges than they had the other nine months previously. But they were something of a different breed. They were mentally stronger and resilient, something most couldn't understand unless witnessed firsthand. It was hard to describe with words, but those who saw them were well convinced of their prowess.

Lin Shin and Shichiro were fierce warriors. They often thought about how they'd had to leave their armor behind before going up the mountain. It was something that they weren't happy about. Would it be something that they would ultimately regret? The answer would reveal itself only in time.

During their first few months living in the mountain, they constantly saw a dark shadow. Something or someone was seemingly always watching them. Someone who never took his beady red eyes off of them. It was truly a very powerful being who lurked in the darkness, which they would soon learn.

They both feared the unknown, an opponent unlike any other they had faced before. The fear grew stronger and stronger, gaining strength over time. Fear itself was an unknown adversary to them, an unfamiliar emotion until the point. They were now parents, though, and protecting their son was the one thing that mattered to them above all else. Something was out there, threatening their son's safety, a creature that may not be human, and this disturbed them greatly.

The Lees steeled themselves against their fear, remembering that they had wiped out hundreds of shoguns before leaving for Okla mountain. They were the best at what they were capable of doing. That was something that the entire land knew, and word traveled fast. Fear of the Lees was instilled among the people.

#

One early spring day, Shichiro took a walk from where they were to the top of Okla mountain. He had told Lin Shin that he was going. She knew he wouldn't have listened even if she tried to tell him no. It was scary for him, even in the more temperate climate of early spring. He had no body armor, and his swords were the only things that were his weapons of choice to offer protection.

Lin Shin hugged him and gave him a small peck on the cheek as he left. She had the fleeting, awful thought that she wouldn't ever see him again. It was a terrifying sense of foreboding that arose from both of their growing concerns.

A sense of evil and darkness, beyond anything that they could understand, hung in the air around them. The source of such power and wrath, which had seemingly been studying and watching them from afar, was none other than the black demon named Orthor, that same very powerful demon that had been locked away by many of Radagast's fellow wizards for thousands of years before him.

Orthor had almost destroyed many lands with his six dark horses that helped him nearly destroy the world, while killing much of the population in it. He was the deadliest of demons. Yet his power was limited, and his curse would not be completely broken for another 400 years.

He had a great deal of power. His beady red eyes gave the sense that death was constantly looking over everyone before him with a fatal stare. He was an angry, imposing figure, standing close to eight feet tall, and very muscular in comparison to any other human or beast. Not even the great Lees would be immune to the fearsome qualities the demon possessed, as they both clearly knew someone or something had been in the shadows, at the window, in the distance, watching them from the top of Okla mountain, the entire time they had been inhabiting it.

Shichiro Lee left plenty of food and supplies that Lin Shin had needed for their son The Master, and her. Meanwhile, Shichiro Lee had embarked on a journey to the top of Okla mountain, which was about a two-day journey from the point of the mountain where they were. It was an entirely possible journey, and besides being cold, he wouldn't face the same hardships, since it was not as arduous a trip as it had been during the winter.

Shichiro Lee was scared as anything, constantly on the lookout for mountain lions and other animals native to Okla mountain. They hadn't really explored too far away from the camp during the winter months, since the conditions were bad, and the chance of survival without one another was very low. But this was just as bad if not worse odds, for Shichiro was by himself and his skill with his weaponry was rusty and out of practice. He held tightly to his two swords for dear life all the same.

There wasn't much that Shichiro wasn't able to do by himself. He was capable of so much more than the average person, but they he and Lin Shin were both still human and did have more human qualities. He knew fear in at least some sense, and so did Lin Shin. Neither of them had truly felt fear that led to any real cost, still, there was now an abundance of it, as he had taken two days to travel up the mountain, stopping a few times to rest and make camp in the places he deemed safe.

Being by himself was dangerous. He didn't have anyone watching his back for safety measures. This was something that Shichiro knew, which caused him to be cautious. He had his fair share of run-ins with some wild animals and had to fight them off with his swords. Only his climbing ability allowed him to stay away from the pack in order to survive. Those these incidents were minor and held him up a bit, they weren't anything that would derail him from ultimately reaching the top of Okla mountain.

At long last, he stood up and pulled himself to the top of the mountain. He was very cautious and his eyes darted around, as his heart raced as if it were about to come out of his chest. When he surveyed his surroundings, he realized it was less the top of a mountain he was looking at, and more of a ruler's point. The mountain top wasn't made of rocks or stone. It seemed that if one managed to survive long enough to get to this point, it was either sheer luck, or the will of whoever it was up on that mountain who wanted that person to live.

Shichiro pulled himself up and stood up, with two swords on his back, and the look of a warrior ready to destroy anyone or anything at any cost. Shichiro Lee squinted, as everything was in darkness, as he'd grown accustomed to throughout Okla and even Okla mountain.

No light existed to shine past the evil and darkness that always lurked from the top of Okla mountain. There was no warm heart to beam out a beacon of hope at the destruction that was almost the end of the world.

Shichiro Lee walked carefully and noticed a seal in the middle of the mountain. There were five images on the seal, as if others had died from his rule. Shichiro inspected it closely and found that it was in a language he couldn't read or understand. He was from the school of the ancient language, an old form of language that hadn't been used for many years.

There was a particular marking on the seal that Shichiro had seen from afar, which interested him. It was hard to see in the darkness, and he took great care, looking around him, as he walked toward it, his swords in both hands.

As he examined it more closely, he saw the image of himself, along with five others on the emblem of metal in the middle of the mountain top, all in gold. It looked so out of place there on the ground. A throne chair wasn't too far off from where the emblem was. It was a monster; Shichiro had just realized that this creature was a monster and beast at the same time.

He turned around, and in the rocks that were scattered around appeared to be images of the dead souls of humans and the remnants of what he had done to them. His heart pounded as if he knew he should have never attempted to reach the top of Okla mountain.

He was very careful and sensed someone was watching him. From out of the darkness came a figure with a large frame and beady red eyes. The black demon was strong and intimidating to behold.

The demon, Orthor, swiftly grabbed Shichiro and slammed him to the ground, as his swords dropped out of his hands.

Orthor stood over the seal, while Shichiro, bereft of his usual weaponry, stood helpless. The demon's strength was far greater than he could have handled. He needed help in order to survive. This was a fight that he wasn't going to win on his own.

He struggled from the tight grasp of Orthor, as his strong hands crushed his ribs.

What he couldn't see was that Lin Shin was just climbing up the mountain in a hood, and she had The Master at her side.

She climbed up and placed The Master behind one of the massive rocks that surrounded the top of the mountain to protect and conceal him as she prepared to do battle. She quietly took out her sword and launched it towards Orthor.

It sliced right through the hulking demon. Shichiro gasped for air as he was released from the creature's grip. He held his ribs and slowly got up, then struggled to run towards Lin Shin.

She ran to get him and helped him stay upright and move closer to her. Shichiro Lee finally leaned against the rock, while Lin Shin grabbed The Master. The little baby looked at Orthor.

"Die!" he cried out, then started to wail again.

At that moment, Orthor detected something within The Lees that he had been waiting and watching for. The reason for his interest related to his own use, which would come to backfire hundreds of years later.

Orthor suddenly raised his arms up. As he did, thick steel bars came up all around the mountain, as if caging the Lees in.

Orthor smiled as he pulled Lin Shin's sword out of his stomach and dropped it. The sound of metal clanged against the ground.

The Lees looked at each other furtively. They knew that they had pissed him off. The Lees had each had a sword, and a wordless sentiment passed between them: this was going to be their roughest fight yet.

As for Orthor, he would have never faced humans who would die trying to kill anyone or anything that would sacrifice their own well-being.

Both of the parents protected their little baby, The Master. This was the one thing that mattered to both of them. They looked at one another, nodded the signal, then charged Orthor with a very intense look. They intended to fight him to the death if necessary.

As the thunderous demon ran towards the two humans, his anger was intense. His huge size and his strength far exceeded what they would normally be capable of handling. The Lees had to think smart in order to outwit the demon, rather than overpower him through sheer force alone. They would need to employ more clever maneuvers.

They both ran towards him, and both of them slid down as they got closer to him. From their knees, they threw out deadly carved knives, which landed in the chest of Orthor.

Orthor had jumped, and while he was midair was exactly the moment his chest was covered in all of the knives, which had been flung at him, rapid-fire, by both of the Lees.

The Lees slid and crashed into the bars that surrounded the top of the mountain. Orthor came down hard beside them with a thunderous impact. His eyes revealed how infuriated he was at that moment. He still struggled to regain all of his strength back from the curse that was hundreds of years from being broken.

The Lees were in agony after having been slammed into the metal, and their faces contorted in pain. Meanwhile, Orthor threw the metal knives down and reset his stance.

The Lees gradually stood up, and they prepared themselves to launch into their combat mode. They set their sights and charged Orthor, speeding toward the tall black demon.

They focused their energy on his feet, in an exhausting battle of speed versus strength.

For a bit, it seemed to be working, though Orthor's strength, his anger, and his aggression were too overwhelming for the both of them. Still, the Lees had managed to get in some critical shots on Orthor, which no one had ever done or lived to talk about ever before. The Lees were human, but he quickly learned that they weren't like anyone that he had seen to this point in any battle.

He carefully regarded them, then walked slowly towards the middle of the mountain top where the emblem lay, illustrating the six dark horses. He looked at them and asked them to hold on to something.

Everything halted, while the Lees stood in confusion. In the midst of their furious battle, suddenly the demon wanted to talk.

"You earned my respect," he pronounced solemnly.

The Lees acted on instinct and grabbed their baby. Lin Shin had made her way to her child and clutched The Master close to her body. Lin Shin and Shichiro both looked at one another, perplexed at this turn of events.

While Orthor began demonic incantations of unknown origin, the sky became as dark as ever. Far in the distance, Radagast realized that it was Orthor who had finally emerged. He looked up and bowed his head. Though he knew that something was happening, he had no idea of the specifics of what transpired so high up on the mountain. As he stood outside his hut with his red hat, he frowned with concern.

Meanwhile, on the mountain top, Orthor continued his creation process, conjuring something as he looked at them both. Then, heavy gusts of winds began to blow with the backdrop of an evil red sky, and lightning that looked as if it were clearly from beyond earth. This force was derived from a strong evil, which had much more power behind it than the warriors had recognized.

Orthor looked at them with a proud but menacing countenance. He had finished, and his creation pleased him. What he had created were the "five scrolls of terror," as he proclaimed them to be, in which he gave the Lees' son, The Master, immortality, in addition to his vast fighting abilities, which he would continue to develop all on his own.

The demon, once foe but now an ally of sorts, walked over towards them with his red eyes gleaming with his secretive purpose. In doing such a deed for the young son of the Lees, he now revealed that he expected them to give him something in return.

Lin Shin thought about it for a few seconds. Wordless sentiments and emotions played out on her face, and she spoke volumes to Shichiro without saying a single syllable out loud. Shichiro nodded, accepting whatever terms she would come up with.

Finally, she spoke.

"You may take the skin from my son, The Master's, skull. Will this satisfy you?"

Orthor looked at her. "Are you certain about this?"

Both Lees bowed their heads, submitting to the terms agreed upon.

Orthor put his large demon hand over The Master's head, instantly vaporizing the skin that covered his skull. As the flesh detached, there was left a blood bath of the remains of the young man's facial bones: the tendons and sinews interwoven into the skeleton part of his head that remained. However, despite the removal of his skin from his head, because he was now immortal and couldn't die, it would not matter what anyone would do. From this point on, he would be practically invincible.

"Why did you want to do this?" asked Shichiro. "Why our son?"

"Because," Orthor gave them a meaningful look, "your son is someone who will change the world. He will be a great warrior, better than the two of you put together. Now, with this new power of immortality, he will be able to fulfill this destiny, without being hindered by human mortality constraints." His head tilted toward the sky. "Legends never die; they only begin!"

With that, his gift of immortality having been bestowed and the five scrolls of terror created, Orthor vanished. From that point on, the Lees never saw him again.

Orthor had lifted the gates so that the Lees could get off the top of Okla mountain. The experience that they had up there was beyond comprehension, and neither one of them could quite understand its meaning or how it would impact the rest of their lives.

Shichiro Lee examined the five scrolls that the demon had wrought. In English, it translated to say that they should not be opened until The Master reached the age of eighteen. Orthor had included within the scrolls the language of the new age, something he would need in the future, besides the words of his own ancient language, which his parents would teach him in time. Soon, all would be revealed.

#

As the years passed, it seemed as if things were beginning to work out in their favor. The Master continued to grow, and his skills were progressing rapidly under the tutelage of the Lees. Despite his young age, he had become a fast learner, and to intensify his overall fierceness, he had a very intimidating look with his eyes, which had now turned red after the demon's touch, and his shiny skull.

The Master looked purely evil. The Lees had trained him in the art of swordsmanship and martial arts, and he had become so good at it, he was ten times better than both of his parents had been at such a young age.

As time went on, their son's evil nature and his strength grew in tandem with one another. His prowess in battle and hand-to-hand combat were unsurpassed, and his personality developed into that of a vicious and unrelenting warrior.

Before long, the Lees recalled that a piece of armor had been left on top of the mountain, which was forged by Orthor. They began to think about that armor and retrieving it for their purposes and for their son.

When the day of The Master's eighteenth birthday came, the family headed up back to the top of Okla mountain, as they had been instructed to do. All three of set off on the journey together, after having packed up everything from their hut.

The top of the mountain was where the demon was, and it was also where they'd been told the powerful armor resided: an armor that could not ever be destroyed by anyone or anything. They also knew, as they had been told so many years ago, that their son would only be able to break Orthor's seal when he stood over the seal of the six dark horses.

The Lees followed the instructions they had been given long ago and proceeded with their plans.

Meanwhile, from a very far distance away, Orthor knew what kind of warrior The Master would become and what type of legend would grow. . .

This was something that Radagast knew as well. They both knew that The Master possessed the ability to become much more dangerous than anything that could come to the surface.

After a two-day journey up to the top of Okla mountain, the Lees and their son, The Master, stood at the peak, where Orthor had created the five scrolls of terror, and just as Orthor had told the Lees, at the age of eighteen, he would now fulfill the instruction to open the scrolls on the emblem.

Now, the time had come for the Lees to leave The Master and go back to Okla. They hadn't any idea what would be waiting for them or anything that had happened in the span of eighteen years' time. They would soon find out.

Radgast hadn't forgotten and nor had Takeo, the head Shogun who had been waiting the same amount of time as well. There was a lot of time, and the Lees couldn't be certain if anything would ever be done, as The Master was told by his parents what was done already and what still remained to be completed. He was a might warrior, and he was of the same mind as the Lees.

At an early age, The Master had been made aware that nothing was ever done without a particular kind of consequence at the same time. Maybe not right away, but over time, those repercusssions would eventually emerge.

The Master now stood, the five scrolls of terror in his hand. Shichiro Lee had handed them over, and then glanced behind him, as they headed back towards the bottom of Okla mountain.

Soon, a heavy fog rolled in at the same time that he grasped the scrolls. It held a mysterious air when, as the Lees disappeared, he held onto the five scrolls of terror that were all wrapped up as one.

He looked around and the heavy darkness, the large clouds, and the mist made him wonder. Slowly, he opened the scrolls and removed the seal.

Heavy rumblings immediately shook the earth. Okla trembled, and the heavy red clouds of what seemed like Hell had finally come. Red lightning filled the sky, painting it the color of lava.

The Master stood with his shiny silver skull gleaming, and his red eyes bursting forth with the same color red that filled the sky. The armor he had found and put on resembled someone of an ancient generation of warriors, a light brown and black pattern that the world had not seen before. This was a creation and gift from Orthor, happily bestowed on the newly immortal man.

It was The Master's armor and his six-foot-three Japanese warrior stature that combined to make him look far more terrifying than both of his parents put together. The Master was not only a frightening sight to behold, but his skills were far better than his teachers, too.

With a red string tied around his armor, this red cloth was a symbol of death and destruction. His strength merely added to the imposing sight of him, as the red lightning and the enormous power had gone directly into his body, delivered there by Orthor. The explosion on top of the mountain and the vibrations and tumbling of many rocks and debris, which fell down Okla mountain, were clear signs that The Master had finally received his power.

It was a moment that Radagast had dreaded, and he bowed his head, as the huge explosions raged, and smoke and destruction filled the air, born from the five scrolls of terror that The Master had finally absorbed.

The Master stood as the smoke gradually dissipated. He kneeled, the rubble and rocks having partially covered him.

He began to move and thrash away the rocks that had covered him. As he did so, the stones split into pieces. His superior strength crushed the hard rocks to bits. Then, he jumped through the broken shards, as if it were nothing. There was now no question that he was stronger than the Lees.

It was time to head back down the mountain and meet up with his parents. It was time to face the world and conquer it. Since the Master was behind his parents by a few days, he knew he had a lot of time to catch up to them. But it was well worth it from everything that The Master had received. The armor from Orthor, in particular, was the most unique thing he had ever seen.

The Master hadn't been around anyone or anything. But as he had started down the mountain of Okla, he knew he had a journey that would be quite far. With one sword from his father and one sword from his mother, The Master's journey was truly just beginning. It was a long trek down the mountain and a solid few days to get to his mother and father. It was a significant journey on foot. He didn't expect to easily catch up to his parents, especially with the aid of horses being a far thought from Japan. They were so far behind the times.

Meanwhile, the Lees had journeyed farther down the mountain toward the entrance. When they reached nearly the midpoint, they hesitated. Something didn't seem right, and they both seemed puzzled. It was alarming on a few accounts. The Lees started to notice things around them that hadn't seen before. They spotted lookout towers that they had seen from a distance on the way down to Okla. Things were slightly amiss, and they felt strongly that things weren't going to be the way that they had anticipated or hoped.

The town seemed built up, and certain things made them wonder; the things that they saw were clear indicators that Okla from the way it had been when they had left. It was inconceivable the changes that had been wrought. Okla itself, however, in terms of atmosphere, was still dark and very gloomy. That feeling of Okla hadn't changed one bit.

The Lees, of course, knew nothing of Radagast, and it was the ancient wizard who had harbored such anger, for the deaths of all those shoguns almost twenty years ago now. His patience while waiting for the time of reckoning grew thin. He knew that at some point, they would eventually have to travel that snowy path in order to get down the mountain. So, he bided his time.

It was common knowledge that Okla had one way up, and one way down. It was always dreary and ill-lit, and from a very far distance, Orthor looked on. The demon had already known their fate, and in the back of his mind, he also knew the fate of The Master. There were things that he had always known, just like Radagast; they both shared that same power. However, he realized that for the things of which he had precognition, it wasn't time just yet. The young man would have to overcome many more things before those culminating events would transpire.

The Lees were very weary of traveling down the mountain on foot. They held their swords in their hand, gracing each step with the sound of their feet stepping in snow. It seemed more intimidating for them, as they didn't know what was coming around each next corner or from out of the surrounding, shrouded area. Of course, the Lees were two deadly fighters and warriors who had once killed clans of shoguns. What would be different this time? Yet, there was a pall cast over the world that lay in front of them, and an irrevocable turn of events, as yet unseen, lurked somewhere in the near future for them.

Radagast's senses were awakened and in tune to the world around him, too. He could feel them headed down the mountain. He sharpened his awareness and knew that it was time. Even though more than twenty years had passed, and in that time he had only gotten a few hours' sleep, he had never stopped thinking about them in all those years.

He got ready, and ran to find Takeo. He woke up the samurai.

The warning was alarmed, and the Lees didn't make much of it, but they were very aware that something was happening.

Before long, a fight was brewing. The Lees were steadily advancing, resolutely, down the mountain, while at the middle of the mountain, a swarm of angry, vengeful shoguns charged to meet them, led by Takeo.

With the sky dawning an evil darkness, a mist unfurled over the land. The Lees knew it was something to pay attention to. Meanwhile, Takeo led the charge up the snowy mountain, and it was immediately evident that the group of shoguns was far greater than those the Lees had killed twenty years ago. They looked at one another with more than a hint of worry, but they had no idea what they were truly up against.

The pure expressions of fear that took over their faces betrayed their inner selves. When stripped of their hardened, warrior exterior, after all, they were just simple human beings, and when confronted when their own mortality, they reacted the same as anyone would. They trembled and steeled themselves for the fight of their lives. Between the very real possibility of perishing at the hands of Takeo, and the dangerous, snowy conditions in the mountain, and Okla itself, they were facing a challenge that would be difficult to overcome, and they would have to draw from as much inner strength as they could muster.

"What do we do?" Lin Shin asked Shichiro.

He nodded at the impending mass of shoguns heading their way and placed a hand on her shoulder.

"We fight, as we have always done," he told her.

"Of course," she responded. "We will do it together."

They looked in each other's eyes, and an expression of determination and resilience passed between them.

The next few moments were a flurry of movement and explosive attacks from both sides, as the shoguns charged and the Lees counteracted each of their movements. The bodies were so much that more than half the mountain was filled with the fury of many shoguns. The fight was overwhelming, and the Lees had to pull out every trick and maneuver that they could think of.

For a few minutes, the Lees thought they might have a chance, as they killed a fair number of the enemy that clambered toward them. But the rows and rows of shoguns just kept coming, trampling toward them. With every blow they suffered, they stood back up to thwart the shoguns, but eventually, they were overpowered and lay on the ground, beaten, bloody, and inches from death.

In one last valiant attempt, Shichiro lifted himself from the ground and sliced the throats of two more shoguns. As he did, six others were upon him and covering him in wounds and bruises, some to his major arteries.

Lin Shin squeezed her eyes shut, as she lay in the snow near her warrior husband. She was bleeding internally and had nothing left in her.

After a furious but fleeting effort, in the end, it was no match, and the Lees were finally killed by Takeo's shoguns, putting a definitive end to a battle that had left many shoguns dead and scattered across the snow, along with two great warriors, the Lees.

Body parts and blood covered the mountainside, pools of red coloring the white snow. It was one part of Takeo's and Radagast's plan, now fulfilled.

Takeo dragged the body of one of the Lees, another shogun dragged the other body, and they left the bodies nailed to the two trees that were side by side. He used their own swords to hold them up by the shoulders.

Rage began to build inside Takeo, and his evil side prevailed, as he thought about the destruction that had been caused by the Lees and The Master. It was as if the deaths of all of his shoguns and all of those before them at the hand of the Lees had instilled in him the need for revenge. The screams from the many deaths and the pain echoed sharply in his mind, and they resonated throughout the mountain.

#

The Master was about a day behind, on foot. The echoes of Okla mountain roared, and he sensed something was terribly wrong. He sensed that it had to do with his mother and father. The Master was young, powerful, and skilled. He was a walking weapon, as great as his mother and father were, yet on a different level of his own, unsurpassed by anyone.

He raced through the snow, with his armor that had been made from scratch. He spent some time working on it, and it was stronger than most anything else. It was crafted from the finest materials; not one sword would be able to even make a scratch on this armor. The Master charged as fast as he could toward the entrance of Okla mountain.

Seeing the red-stained snow, and the dead bodies of the shoguns, he frantically cast his eyes all around, hoping that none of the blood belonged to his parents. They were nowhere in sight. He was concerned, as any son would be. His eyes were inflamed with fury. That was an emotion that could have dangerous consequences now, when it came to The Master. A warrior and a lethal weapon, the sight of him was sure to evoke fear in anyone who would see him.

He stood on the mountain, as night drew in, and Takeo stood at the bottom, looking out. Through the heavy mist, Takeo was taken aback by what he beheld. It was The Master, a warrior that he would never have expected to see: a skull with no skin, red eyes, glowing in anger. He stood, awestruck at what type of warrior The Master had become.

It was the stuff of legends, already in the making, and not the good kind. The Master let his feet fall heavily with each stride, and with his two swords in his hands, he was angry and puffing as if his one focus was to kill everything and anything that stood in his way.

Takeo looked on, as a large number of shoguns raced towards him. A great number of them had fled, in fear of the ghastly sight of The Master. Covered in armor and body gear, he didn't look like any type of shogun. He was something much more powerful than Takeo or even Radagast could have ever envisioned. His presence was beyond terrifying, and there were no words that could describe the effect he had as he marched forward toward the mass of shoguns.

As he ran towards the middle of Okla mountain, he did not let the wet snow impede his step. With his two swords out, a fleet of nearly one hundred shoguns met him. They had been sworn to protect Takeo and Radagast. The large number of furious shoguns didn't seem to have any impact on the speed with which The Master continued his march. Nothing could slow down his deadly trajectory. His swordsmanship and his powerful swings with both hands were the worst things that anyone could have seen at that moment.

Without hesitation, The Master began to kill anyone and everything that approached him. There was not one weapon that could even get close to him. The Master had the numbers stacked against him, but his martial arts were so much greater than anyone that they had ever seen. Even topping his own parents, he was ten times better than they could have ever wished to be.

The Master cut through anything that walked, by the fury of his swings with his freshly cut blades. He was so much stronger, and even his kicks and other maneuvers far surpassed anyone who tried to stop him. His speed and strength were simply unparalleled

It was only a matter of time before The Master had killed everyone in his way. The young warrior was covered in blood from his skull to his feet. Okla mountain, too, was covered in red from the snow to the rocks, which had heads bashed upon them, blood from all the shoguns. Other body parts lay scattered all over the widely spread Okla mountain. There was nothing left of the shogun army that Radagast thought would have stopped The Master. It was impossible to foresee this outcome, but they should have, since The Master came from the Lees, two of the deadliest warriors that Japan had ever seen.

The Master surveyed the destruction he had caused, and the sight fueled his evil heart even further, leaving a void; he was without caring and craved nothing except the kill. In fact, now that he had a taste for blood, he killed as if it were a sport, and he was very good at it.

The Master now faced Takeo, who stood frozen in shock, unwilling to believe the truth that The Master had wiped out all of the shoguns that he had. He was scared now for his own life, observing The Master's swords were completely soaked in red. Takeo's fear was evident.

Takeo continued to look on, as The Master trampled over some of the bodies, leaping over them to reach Takeo. Takeo stood in shock at his prowess and agility.

The Master and Takeo fought. Quickly, Takeo discovered that he could not outmaneuver The Master, and his ability and power were unmatched. Anything that Takeo threw at him was a laughable joke to the poised and skilled warrior.

The Master toyed with Takeo, after a series of back and forth swings. The Master dropped his two swords, and used all of his skillful power moves, beating him senseless with a series of forceful and agile movements, using his arms, his legs, and his strength to plow into Takeo and deliver him brutal blows. It was an excruciating event for Takeo, beyond any pain he'd felt before. Takeo was thrown, punched, and knocked off his feet over and over. There wasn't one move that The Master couldn't have done, that Takeo could have avoided.

He finally grew weary of dominating Takeo so easily, and with one easy motion, The Master delivered one final, fatal kick to his neck, which decapitated his entire head from his body. Takeo's head rolled away while blood spurted, and his body collapsed to the ground.

The Master stood directly in front of Takeo's body and smiled. Meanwhile, the town had been deserted, as the people had run to protect their families, and some shoguns ran from the mountain as well. It was a risk not worth taking.

The houses looked as if a stampede had run savagely throughout the village, and there wasn't too much left standing from the destroyed houses, and everything that had been broken by people running for dear life upon seeing who and what was coming. Debris and wreckage was strewn about from the chaos.

The Master had instilled fear in the people's hearts, and seeing what he looked like was enough to cause that reaction. He stood in what was left of Okla, surveying the death and the destruction from the people running, and the pain that he had administered to all the shoguns that he had killed. He knew there was more to this slaughter than that.

The Master was wise, and smart. Still, his anger overtook him. He wandered around and found one person in the village who was still alive, and others who had hidden, as they couldn't flee in time.

Roughly, The Master grabbed the boy, who had to be in his mid-teens.

The Master examined him, as he lifted him up off the ground. The boy trembled in fear, as he was slowly brought eye-level with the frightening skull of The Master.

The young boy covered his eyes and whimpered.

The Master looked at him with a menacing gaze and demanded, "Who put the hit on my parents?"

The boy continued shaking in abject terror. He knew this furious warrior wasn't about to ask twice, so he lifted his head up and pointed.

"Over the hill," he said in a quaking stutter, "T-t-there is a hut with a wizard. His name is Radagast." The sight of the skinless Japanese warrior with red eyes staring at him would have haunted him in his dreams for years to come.

The Master, however, would not let him live long enough to have those nightmares. He put him back down, and promptly snapped his neck, killing him instantly.

He took off running in the direction where the boy had pointed, and as he did, Orthor looked down on the turn of events from the top of Okla. *He is a killing machine. I will have to keep an eye on him*, the large black demon thought, as he continued to observe, waiting to see what would transpire next.

\#

He started to run through the heavy snow, and with each step, he drew closer and closer to Radagast, and he could feel that exacting his revenge was within his reach. It was a fate that Radagast had accepted and had to go through the motions of fulfilling. It was something that he knew instinctively had to happen.

The Master sprinted towards the hut, and his way was lit by a candle burning in the window, as the boy had told him. The body count from The Master's killing spree was a few hundred shoguns, whom he had either killed or left bloodied. He stood on the top of the hill, looking down, as he thought there would be another group of shoguns waiting to protect Radagast.

Carefully, he proceeded on his path. He was well aware that he was now going to approach a wizard who had magic and powers unknown to him or to his parents, abilities in which he had not been trained. When The Master finally reached the hut, he stood outside and looked around quietly, pensively. He contemplated what he did not understand about this so-called magic. What was it? What could it do?

Radagast stood inside. He used his only defense against the powerful warrior; he began to speak, as he was beginning a spell to cast on The Master. While he knew he couldn't kill this great warrior because of the five scrolls of terror, which gave him the power of invincibility and immortality, he could at least bind his power and limit his ability to do harm. This would prove very useful. Radagast knew The Master couldn't be killed, and he knew his fate was already sealed.

The door was blocked, an attempt to keep The Master out. He tried to gain access to the small hut, and for an instant, the barrier worked. However, it was only a matter of time, as the wind began to pick up very heavily, the clouds became dark blue, and fierce rain came down like someone was attempting to alter the elements and the air around them.

Next, lightning began to strike in an unnatural trajectory, and it hit The Master several times; the direct contact did not faze him one bit. He was strong and getting angrier by the second.

Radagast's next move was to bring to life creatures from a far-off dimension to try to stop The Master, large beasts with sharp teeth and brute strength. Again, it was impossible to stop him, and the warrior easily plucked off the onslaught of creatures and crushed them. Eventually, the pack of beasts were killed and lying in a bloody heap, just like the shoguns had been.

After The Master had killed everything and anything that was thrown at him, he picked up one of the animal skulls and hurled it at the door to the hut, easily splintering it apart and collapsing it inward.

Radagast, now exposed from the broken door, had his book in front of him, and he began a new incantation, a spell that would freeze The Master forever, preventing him from doing any more harm to man or beast.

A tingling sensation took over The Master's extremities. Then, he felt stiffness in his legs and had the vague feeling that some type of material was coated around his limbs, rendering them immobile. The Master was quickly losing his ability to move, as his arms and legs became completely paralyzed.

The Master cried out in fury, as he knew something was happening and that it was connected to the words that Radagast was saying.

"I don't want to die!" he howled. But would there be a chance that he wouldn't? Maybe there was a chance that this wouldn't happen at all as he had thought.

Radagast held out hope for his own part that his words would hold the proper power and that the effect of the spell would create the desired circumstances. However, he, too, wondered if things would change.

The Master looked helpless and he began to worry, as Radagast appeared cautiously triumphant. He had a feeling that his short-lived reign of terror, and the legacy of his family name was about to come to an end. The Master had only a slight bit of movement left in his arms. Otherwise, Radagast had successfully encased the rest of his body in the spell.

While Radagast murmured the final words in the incantation, suddenly The Master used an overpowering amount of strength in his arm and broke free in surprising fashion.

Radagast was shocked and stood there, mid-sentence, stunned.

In one sharp, quick motion, The Master raised his right arm and threw the bloodied sword right through the heart of Radagast, killing him, and stopping him from completing the spell that would have frozen The Master forever.

With his last breath, barely able to articulate a single syllable, the wizard attempted to complete the spell. Instead, he slurred his words in the agony of dying, and instead of freezing the warrior forever, what he ended up saying in his inarticulate state was "400 years" in Japanese. This was a great misfortune for Radagast, as he had hoped to put a stop to the cycle of bloodshed. Now he had only temporarily delayed it.

Radagast was laid against a bookcase where he had The Master's sword still penetrating through his heart. He was at last dead, having fulfilled his unavoidable destiny.

Radagast had not completed the original spell, and now there was in place a spell that would only last 400 years. A great wind swooped away Radagast and destroyed the house in the process. The remains of the wizard were later collected into the Urn of Symboltos. As the wizard burned to ashes and his remains found their way into the urn, all the rest of the surroundings were swept away by the heavy tornado that came swirling in from the middle of nowhere, unexpectedly.

The town of Okla was completely destroyed and the only thing that was left in the wake of the final showdown by The Master and the wizard was dirt. Okla had become a wasteland from the tornado. It was so hard to even imagine or understand what had truly happened, never mind deciphering the reasons why it had. There was barely anyone left alive, no survivors who had suffered the experiences firsthand anyway; only those few families remained who had been on the outskirts of the town, and they were the ones to pick up the wreckage. One of those families secreted away the Urn of Symboltos, without understanding what was inside, but for all intents and purposes, the wizard was gone, and the whereabout of his remains was unknown to most. This was the way everything was supposed to happen, as it would only be a matter of time when these things would come up again. In fact, it would only be 400 years later when The Master would have to be reckoned with once again.

The Master was not dead, as he had been frozen into a statue that was made out of iron. That was the only thing that remained in Okla and had withstood the tornado. Still, after the last couple of families had fled the town, no one was left alive or aware of what had happened there. Everyone in the land of Japan knew of the Lees and The Master, but no one had any evidence what had ever happened to the Lees. They simply had heard that the Lees had been killed.

As the months passed since Radagast had disappeared, there was a growing fear among Japan that The Master wasn't dead. Some even began to fear that The Master still lurked in the wreckage of Okla and would soon strike again. Too many people feared going into Okla since what had happened, and the roads were not in passable condition, so there would be no way of knowing for certain the fate of The Master. There was nothing that even the greatest warrior or even any citizen could have done.

The Master soon became a legend, and not a good one, either. He had put fear in the eyes and minds of everyone. The Master had a curse on him, but so, too, did the town of Okla.

Chapter 4

Five years had passed since everything had transpired involving The Master and the destruction of Okla. Haru was a family leader shogun, who lived in close proximity to Okla in a village called Hirshima. One night he held a meeting in the town circle.

"I realize," he began, "that there has been a great fear of Okla, and I know we are not too far from that town. Some of you feel that the town has been cursed, haunted, or whatever other stories you may have heard..."

He went on speaking, but the response was merely whispered accounts that simply furthered the myths, entrenching the people in their fear.

The villagers all knew the story of the Lees and The Master. None knew how much of it was true, but the legends lived on. It was making the people of Hirshima village worried and scared to even go outside even during certain traditional events; some even hesitated to leave their houses for ordinary reasons. This began to be a very large concern for a new leader of one of the newer shogun's families. He was rational and thought predominantly with logic-based reasoning, not listening to the wild, exaggerated tales about curses.

The town was filled with approximately forty families, mostly young people. There was fear, and as each tradition was set at night, there was never an abundance of people who would be in attendance. It had made Haru very frustrated and alarmed to a point where he had to understand why so many people weren't coming out for their traditions. He had to figure out the root cause.

Haru had thought long and hard, in his quarters, about his concern for his clan. His wife didn't understand why this was happening either, but it was alarming. He slept on it one night, and it kept him up for most of the night.

His thoughts stirred him in the middle of the night; he looked out of the window, and the darkness that seemed to pour in alluded to something greater that was coming. He sensed that it was some type of evil, even greater than The Master. It occurred to Haru that perhaps a meeting in the afternoon around noon would be much more feasible for the people of Hirshima village, and perhaps then they would listen to reason, when exposed to the harsh light of day, instead of cloaked in the mysterious atmosphere of night.

By the time morning came, Haru had deliberated and knew that this was the only way his people of Hirshima village would come out to the center of town and listen to the leader. Hirshima village was the closet to Okla village, and still, even in other clans much farther away, everyone was terrified to even make trades with anyone near Okla, which only hurt the commerce and the means to thrive within Hirshima village.

Haru alerted his people by having his tower lookout make the announcement. Soon, the word spread so that all the people knew to come to the town circle at noon. Attendance was mandatory, as he had to make decisions and initiate conversations about his idea, which he hoped would stop this fear of The Master and everything involved with Okla.

Haru waited patiently as noon approached; after another half hour passed, finally, he looked around and observed that he had gotten the response he had been waiting for. He stood there with poise and composure and prepared to speak.

With a firm, strong voice, he began. He talked about his many concerns, including his people not following the rules of the town, and the curse that had been worrying him, but most concerning to him was the fact about his people not following the rules that he had put forth. They were a younger clan, but a terrified one at that.

"Since we are near a water canal," Haru said, "I need three volunteers to go into Okla, locate the statue of The Master that we have heard exists, and then move it."

After Haru finished his instruction, there was dead silence; you could hear a pin drop. This was a task for which it would be nearly impossible to get volunteers. As Haru conducted the meeting, he had been surveying the crowd, hoping to find some worthy volunteers or candidates for the difficult task. Even when he prompted them, not one person spoke up to accept the job, nor would anyone want to.

While Haru kept talking, trying to entice someone to volunteer for the job, three strangers had walked into

Hirshima village. They were loners and vagabonds who traveled around Japan. As the three men approached the town circle, they went closer and closer to the town's center, where Haru, their shogun clan leader, was talking.

Kaito, Sora, and Reo were the three travelers who came forward, after hearing the murmurings of the task that was being requested. They had no prior knowledge about Okla, nor The Master, and to them, it did not seem to be an impossible task at all.

They engaged in conversation from the crowd, addressing Haru.

"If you can offer a predetermined amount of money in exchange, we will move it," Kaito said. Sora and Reo nodded in agreement. They were all of the same mind that this would be a simple job with a high reward.

Haru had tried to avoid offering money, but most of his village people wouldn't come forward to take the job and move the statue either. Finally, he weighed his options and took it upon himself to accept the travelers' offer, giving them 500 yens to move the statue of The Master. All of the other villagers breathed a sigh of relief.

Haru left the meeting with the men and showed them where they could sleep for the night. Additionally, they were given a place to store their belongings, and some extra supplies. These would come in handy for all sort of different jobs, so they were pleased.

After the meeting had dispersed, Kaito followed Haru in order to be shown the way to Okla village. Haru pointed out where the statue was. On the way, Kaito remarked that the path to Okla was deserted and dark. Haru remained silent but agreed, and the longer they walked, the more he was persuaded that the fear his villagers had felt was, indeed, warranted. He, too, was now afraid of going into Okla.

Haru showed them the village of Okla, and the three men didn't seem too disturbed about what Haru and his people had felt. Haru turned back toward his own village, while Kaito remained there. He knew his way back from the path Haru had shown him. After Haru had long been departed, Kaito, along with his other two traveling companions, had retrieved the statue.

They grabbed their supplies and took the time to put the statue on a wooden base, with wheels. Haru had a boat that was by the dock that they could load it onto without too much difficulty. It had taken them a few hours to move it, and transport it, then finally to load it onto the boat. Kaito and the other two men worked together to load it securely. Meanwhile, Haru watched and assisted the men in order to get rid of the statue as quickly as possible. Haru knew where they would be moving it to, but Kaito was never given this information. Most people would think to ask, but not Kaito; his only concern was with getting paid.

The next morning, Kaito, Sora, and Reo had rested up in preparation for the great trip. They met with Haru, who was anxiously pacing around, waiting for their arrival beside the boat. He was pleased to see the statue still securely in place and ready for its journey far away from his village to a distant part of the world. Soon, it would finally leave him, and his villagers, in peace.

On the dock, the captain was told by Haru where he was meant to take the statue. But, back then, it was essentially a death sentence. The captain knew in his heart that Haru knew what he was doing. He was doing the right thing for his people; it was about getting the villagers over their constant fear, so that they could go on to live happy, carefree lives. This was the one thing that he had to do. Once his people knew that the statue was far away from Okla and going to be shipped out at any cost, they would be relieved and grateful. Then, they would be a true clan again, fostering the spirit of camaraderie and fellowship, taking part in their community without worries of being torn apart by an unseen predator lurking in the distant town.

Haru spoke to the captain of the boat, and the captain took that death sentence, as he knew there was no turning back, and he was a noble sort of man. They were headed for a place that no boat had ever left the area in search of. Boats typically only went short distances, and even those could be treacherous, let alone on such a long journey that would take months and months to complete. Even if they got to their destination, at what cost would it be for all of those men?

The captain knew that no matter what, he had to get there: New Amsterdam. It was so hard to imagine, since it was on the other side of the world. A distance that seemed so far away, and all those obstacles that could arise along the way. Still, the captain had plenty of food supplies, and things that they would all need for this journey, so they were as prepared as they could be. On average, it would take approximately six months and a great deal of conditioning in order to survive the journey.

As it turned out, the trip would go wretchedly over the six-month period. One by one, each of the crew was battling sickness and other things that couldn't be cured or aided over 400 years ago.

It had made the trip a bit more challenging. The money was good, but was that incentive enough? Was it worth it to have to endure the fierce weather conditions and the changeable, choppy water? Would making the trip of 6,000 miles to New Amsterdam truly be worth it?

For Haru, it was. The three strangers had been paid a considerable sum, and the captain had received his share as well. Even if all else failed and they perished at sea, the statue would be well far away from where it would be in the land of Japan. It was the only way to regain the people's trust, and to get rid of the statue at the same time. There was so much to consider and not enough time to think about it. But Haru did what had to be done in order to best care for his own clan. This exemplified what a true leader he was.

Haru had known that not one of them he would ever see again. After all, it was a death wish, but they all took the money and were happy with the amount that they had been given to take on this suicide mission. It was nothing short of brave.

Months passed, and one by one, each of them got sick, being taken over by illnesses that were not curable at the time, even minor infections or the common cold could escalate and lead to death. They hadn't any medicine but just enough food that had been calculated to last for the months and many miles left to traverse. The important part of the quest was getting the statue to the place where it was intended to go. Often, the crew tried to imagine what was in this statue and why it had to be moved so far away.

Even during the journey, the captain had often wondered, seeing his crew dying one by one, getting sick, weak and throwing up, about the ultimate outcome of this journey. It appeared as if he would be the only one who would make it to New Amsterdam. Would he truly be the only survivor, he wondered?

More time passed, and after many months on the water, he continued to watch the crew members die. There wasn't much food or resources left, and there was still some time left in the journey. The captain found himself feeling weaker and his energy level more and more depleted as the days passed.

As the boat approached a port, he seemed lucky, but he was still very sick. The others had not seen too many Japanese men from what seemed so far away. He didn't understand the language that they were speaking in New Amsterdam. The native language of English was standard, but the captain talked to the boat master and got someone who tried to help translate. They obtained help in moving the statue off the boat and towards a park that seemed to be placed in the center of a surrounding area that appeared like it was being built up all around.

New Amsterdam seemed to have a lot of projects being worked on, and a few of the men who had helped the captain get to the area spoke to the English men about the large park that was being cultivated. They determined the location where it might be possible to place the statue. In fact, the men thought it could actually serve as the centerpiece of the new project's landscape. Before long, it was officially decided, and the statue would soon be the first statue that would be placed down. The rest of the park would be built around it.

The captain proceeded with having the statue unloaded from the vehicle where it was tethered. The men saw that the captain was weak. He suddenly collapsed, looking ashen and trembling. Blinking, his sight beginning to fade as death overtook him, he managed to see through his hazy vision the statue being planted and put into the ground at last.

The Master's statue was in what would later become Central Park. The captain had followed through on his promise. The Master was in what would become New York City. The captain soon died, and all the money had come out of his pockets. It would now be only a matter of years before everyone would find out just what was in that statue.

Chapter 5

It had been more than 400 years, maybe longer, since The Master had been frozen by the curse of Radagast. It had been so long that not too many knew anything about the events that had happened long ago. The people of New Amsterdam certainly had no prior knowledge of it, nor did the people of the Western hemisphere at large. There were those who cared and a group called the Triads was started in Okla, Japan fifty years after the curse and the events of Okla had taken place. There were events that had destroyed the way Japanese life was lived. It had changed their ways and their lifestyle for all time because of those events that had occurred 400 years ago.

It was Halloween weekend in Manhattan. It was nearing nighttime, and a storm looked as if it was looming in the distance, a storm that no one could begin to imagine nor understand. New York had been rocked by terrorist attacks of September 11th. It was now about to experience something on that same level of threat and damage. A cluster of meteorologists converged and murmured about the strange, dark red color in the sky, and the freak bouts of intense lightning storms that seemed to come out of nowhere and go against nature. The experts were puzzled and couldn't quite figure out what was transpiring, since there had been no warning signs or weather patterns to indicate wind or rain, yet the forces of nature now raged before their very eyes. Meanwhile, the people prepared for the parade to take place in downtown Manhattan. The crowds assembled as the authorities did as well as they could to limit any crimes being committed.

In Central Park, there were two gangs about to battle it out with knives. The red tinge had gradually overtaken the sky, and then the colors deepened and spread even further, creating a dark red cloud over the entire city. It appeared as if Hell had broken open over the city. Cars stopped as people gazed up toward the ominous sky. Whether people were in their homes, out on the streets, or stopped in rush-hour traffic, they couldn't help but to stop and stare at the sky above.

The sky darkened even more, and it appeared as dark as midnight or later, as if time had suddenly stood still, at 6 p.m. What was going on with the sky? People asked themselves or each other, looking for answers, but no one had any idea.

Lightning bolts of hot red suddenly began to shoot down towards the people of the city, and sent people running in terror. The terrifying bolts blew up cars, destroyed buildings, and burned a few people alive from the heat on impact. The city immediately went into a total and extreme mode of panic from this. Crowds were running in all directions, as they knew something dangerous was on the verge of happening. What or whom it was, not one of the curious people of New York could speculate. All they knew was that a complete destruction from the red lightning had occurred, but for now, the origins of the lightning were unknown.

Meanwhile, authorities approached the two gangs in Central Park, and they knew something was going to happen, as it had been months since they had been trying to stop these two gangs.

All of a sudden, a massive lightning bolt hit the statue that had to be older than the dirt that had become Central Park. It had been there as long as anyone had ever been populating the city. An echoing sound sent waves throughout the city, piercing the air. As if Manhattan needed something else in its history. All of the city-dwellers heard a screeching bolt descending at a rapid pace, and they all ran for cover. A large iron statue had been hit, and the statue was instantly shattered apart, a long crack forming down its middle, which began to grow.

Everyone slowly got up in a daze, stunned after trying to run for cover from the hot red lightning. The red lighting had disappeared from the sky, as if nothing had ever happened. But it was only the beginning.

More cracks began to spider out all over the iron statue. The two different gang members stood up one by one, and the police did as well. They all looked at one another in disbelief, then turned to see the iron statue being broken open, piece by piece.

They all had guns in hand. The police swiftly surveyed the crowd of people, a fair amount of nearly fifty: the fifteen members of each gang, and twenty police officers that had surrounded this statue. They all knew that something was frozen in this statue, but what? No one knew.

It was shocking and frightening, as no one would have expected it to be possible that anyone could be locked inside of such a statue for almost 400 years, and still survive. As piece by piece broke off from the statue, a leg broke free, followed by an arm that moved slowly, and finally, with a twist of his upper body, the remainder of the statue fell away and dropped to the ground, revealing what had lurked inside.

A warrior had broken free.

A red-eyed warrior stepped out, with no skin on his head and an outfit that only a Japanese warrior could wear. He didn't look like anything depicted in books or paintings, and his appearance was beyond any words to properly describe him. He was much more terrifying than could be put into words. He looked around and clutched his two swords in his hands, a gleam of hatred and disgust in his eyes and his facial movements. His body language and expression could not have been any clearer. He wanted revenge.

The night had finally come, and so had The Master. He started twirling his swords as if he were in battle mode. His skeleton face and head was intimidating enough just to look at, and his red eyes were scary enough to fend off any enemy who merely glanced at him.

After a moment's hesitation, the fifty people opened fire on him, at least those who had guns. What they did not realize, though, was how the 400-hundred-year-old armor that was given to him by his parents, which Orthor had made for him, was indestructible. Every bullet bounced off of him, as if he were a god. He wasn't one, but he was as close to it as anyone could get, with his immortal powers and other abilities bestowed upon him by a demon.

As soon as the smoke cleared, The Master stood and looked around. With the many powers that Orthor gave him, he could adapt to any surroundings and any language. This ability would come in handy, since he had last interacted with other people 400 years ago.

The Master stood and smiled at them with a menacing, evil look in his eyes, and he spoke so that everyone could hear his voice booming out.

"I am The Master! Hear my roar."

He leaped towards them with his two swords; as fast as he was, there wasn't one gang member who could hurt him at all, seemingly, as he jumped with great agility around the large group of fifty. Those who witnessed the bullets bounce off of his armor were shocked.

Each member charged him, one by one, and each one was immediately sent flying from the incredible impact of his punches and kicks and various other skill moves, not to mention the fierce thrusts of his swords, which he wasn't afraid to use.

He was fearless, and conversely, the others were filled with abject terror. The screams from Central Park were loud and painful. Blood began to fill the park, as The Master's swords began to cut and kill each of the fifty people in the park.

They had all tried to stop such a vicious warrior, but there wasn't anything that anyone could have done to slow him down whatsoever. Not one gun or knife had hurt him on any level.

As the death toll climbed, The Master's swords had both cut all the men, and every swipe of blood consumed the blades of his two swords, coating them in the gore. Blood had covered the grass and what was left of the iron statue. It covered the dirt, the trees, the bushes, the benches, even the metal garbage cans that were scattered in the area.

The Master himself was a bloody mess from all the blood that had come out of the bodies from those he had cut open. Screams of death and pain rang out, which were omitted from those who ran from the terror that he had caused by his attack. There wasn't one body left alive after he had killed all of the fifty members of the group in Central Park.

As he began to walk out of the park, many tried to deter him from his course; however, he was no match for anyone who tried to stop him. He broke legs, or ripped legs or arms off with his bare hands. He broke people's necks. He was an impossible force to stop. His strength, his ability was nothing that anyone could ever begin to understand on any level. Each body that approached him, he dropped or used his sword to kill in one of his many skilled ways. Whether it be with his hands, or by using his swords, there was no shortage of methods he could use to kill a human being.

While the evil red-eyed samurai walked out into the streets, the body count continued to grow. The crowds had run, and on Halloween night, he wasn't one of the many who had dressed up as a monster. He *was* the monster, and a warrior whom everyone had run from. A full panic mode set in and swept through the streets like an epidemic of fear. The Master was among what he said he was, a true Master at everything. He was vicious and he was deadly. He was everything that one could ever imagine, and beyond. He left a trail of destruction to those he encountered along his path.

Cars had stopped short in front of him, and as they did, The Master punched right through the hood all the way to the bottom, destroying the engine in an unprecedented way. It was something that was unbelievable. To think that this was happening at this time, in this manner, and in this city. Why would this happen, and why would this person, or being, or whatever plague had descended upon them come *here*, the people witnessing the events wanted to know. But there would be no answers amidst the chaos.

The Master stood near the entrance of Central Park, where people fled, and the authorities had run towards. It wasn't something that a police officer would normally want to run towards. The Master faced civilian after civilian, each one thinking themselves brave enough to fight, and they died seconds after approaching him as well. Most weren't that bold, and near the entrance to Central Park was complete havoc. Innocent people were trampled over, people were dying, cars were being crashed into. Most were in survival mode, doing whatever they needed to do in order to prevail in this situation that they had never encountered before. The streets were in the midst of one warrior's rampage of terrorizing an entire city. He had instilled fear in all those who lived in the city, and news of the events was already beginning to travel.

Businesses shut their doors and locked them. Whatever people had to do after seeing this fearsome warrior, who created so much chaos, was completely understandable. The city near Central Park looked liked a war zone. It was an incredible sight to see the destruction that had filled the city. There hadn't been many police officers that had been left alive after confronting him either. Many had died, or at least were brutally hurt and on the verge of death. There wasn't one person who could have survived any meeting with the fury of the fearsome warriro. He was deadlier than anything or anyone that the police force had ever had to reckon with.

Halloween was an utter disaster. The bodies, the smoke from the destruction, the fires raging in the buildings, and broken glass from windows and storefronts littered the streets. The fires that raged from the lower east side illuminated the night. The Master had gone on a rampage, destroying everything and anything that was in his path. The only problem was that no one could have stopped him, nor was anyone capable of preventing this from happening. It was a deadly situation. It wasn't as if a warrior of his ability woke up every day in a different era, either. The Master's level of destruction was quite visible, and all the dead cops that had tried to stop him were painful reminders and warnings of The Master's power. Fathers, mothers, daughters, and sons. They were all killed by The Master. For his part, The Master had no heart or remorse towards anyone.

#

Halloween had been ruined for this year, and the bodies were strewn all over. The city now prepared for a massive cleanup from that terrible night. Meanwhile, The Master had disappeared into what remained of the night, as the light began to dawn a new day. The early papers of New York City had all read "Halloween Massacre."

The sun began to creep up the sky, and the reporters had been out early; in Central Park, police had been all over this story, and as they should be. They were certainly wary of this unknown assailant, but they still had to do their job as well. Most knew that there was a very loose cannon out there somewhere, and he was not in any uniform whatsoever. It wasn't a person in costume; it was something and someone much more lethal and touched by a curse or something along those lines, they mused.

Captain Thomas pulled up in his cruiser, Lieutenant Jack Rider alongside him. They were the first two to arrive on the scene in the city streets. The smell hit them immediately; the bodies reeked, mixing with the pollution and scent of garbage that permeated the air.

As they both emerged from the vehicle and surveyed the scene, it was a devasting sight to behold, to say the least, and with the taped off crime scene already roped off from the others, the effect of arriving into such surroundings was shocking. The reporters had already been set up far away from the scene. But, the bodies in the street were scattered, so it wasn't hard to see a large team was working all over to search for evidence. The body count and blood was ubiquitous, leaving a sure trail to the source of the destruction.

Captain Thomas was a large, heavyset black man. He had two adoptive sons, Matt and Jack. He had taken in both boys when they were around the age of six, after their parents were killed by a gangster, while they were just walking on the streets. Captain Thomas was young then, and at that point, he and his wife were having trouble conceiving. The tragedy turned into a fortuitous opportunity that just happened to fall into their hands. He saved the young kids' lives, and at the time, the Captain was just a regular police officer. But he had saved their lives, Matt and Jack, and this was a true turning point in both his career and his personal life.

Matt's life had more of a complex beginning with the police force. But, at this particular point in time, it really wasn't a concern to Captain Thomas, unfortunately. Captain Thomas got out of the car with Jack, realizing something severe had happened to the city, as he looked all around and saw the pigeons flying wildly.

Jack, too, looked up and caught a glimpse of something on one of the buildings with dark red eyes looking down at Captain Thomas, leering with a very dark and evil look. It had lasted a few seconds, and as quickly as he had seen it, in another instant, what he had seen was gone.

The stare that The Master had fixed on Captain Thomas seemed like it would have lasted an eternity. But, as brief as it was, the smell and the carnage and the high body count of dead gang members and dead policemen and policewomen took his attention away from anything else.

Captain Thomas couldn't believe it, and nor could Matt's brother Jack. Captain Thomas had walked and immediately doubled over, retching. He cupped his hands over his mouth. Jack gritted his teeth and pressed on, but he could barely stand to walk through all the dead bodies that were littered haphazardly all over the street. Most of the news reporters couldn't even begin to film anything, as the scene was much more gruesome than they could have imagined. Not even the worst horror villains could have done what The Master had done.

There were many factors still unknown, and the police, had no knowledge of anything: who this person was, or where he came from, not to mention the motive he might have had for committing these atrocities. Captain Thomas was deeply concerned, as the city was worried for their safety in a city that never sleeps. This was something far more dangerous than was imaginable. The city-dwellers took comfort in the fact that there wasn't anyone like him, so if he did reappear to continue his rampage, he would be very easily spotted. It wasn't as if he could hide in a crowd.

Still, there was no one alive that had known about The Master, or his story. Captain Thomas knew it would be quite difficult to understand anything about this perpetrator. Maybe he wasn't from around here. But much remained to be learned about his origins at this point.

The aftermath would involve a major cleanup effort, while the city mourned the loss of so many fallen police officers, both men and women. Captain Thomas didn't know where to begin. The bodies that were laid across the streets and in the parks were difficult to capture on film; the yellow police tape prevented anyone from obtaining video footage. The blood and guts of men and woman who had tried to stop The Master was everywhere. Nothing so gruesome had transpired since the shoguns who had tried to stop him over 400 years ago. The Master seemed stronger and smarter than he had so long ago. In some way, he had become wiser. There was no clear way of determining how someone like him had survived after being frozen for so long.

Captain Thomas had a lot to tackle and dig into. It was hard to research something, though, that hadn't really been around or existed at any point in the last 400 years. It wasn't as if he could look up any real details. It was nearly impossible to figure out an entry point of where in the world he was even going to find anyone who might know of this strange and sinister figure. The internet hadn't been around to capture The Master's history, leaving so much undocumented and unknown. Since Okla had been wiped out in the tornado, not even oral traditions had carried on the story.

There was a lot that Captain Thomas had to think about. Maintaining the safety of the city would prove to be a challenge. Meanwhile, the city was plastered with front-page stories, which soon got national attention. One paper in particular reached sensation status: the *Long Island Newsday*. One of the guys there had been shot, and it showed up in the newspaper the next day. Quickly, The Master became more famous than anyone in the country's history. No person, group, or terrorist faction even came close to being as terrifying as he was. The newspaper had a clear picture of him, obtained secretly by a crafty photographer who risked his safety, managing not to be seen or victimized by The Master.

The fall season would last many long weeks. Captain Thomas had spent hours and hours with Jack and many others. It was time that Captain Thomas went back to the precinct: everything was in a state of upheaval, as if a war was raging. Destruction of the city was shown on every news station. Blood still stained the streets. It was heart-wrenching to see the women and men laid in body bag after body bag.

Even the gang members as well. There were truly no words to describe what he had seen.

The tears, combined with barely contained rage was palpable from the survivors on the police force. They were perturbed that no one had any idea of who or what they were up against, and so far, there were no concrete leads or research that had amounted to anything. As much as Captain Thomas was angry, this was someone or something that couldn't be underestimated. It was hard to gauge or find weaknesses for something previously unknown.

In the age of the internet, news generally traveled fast around the world: pictures and videos were already ubiquitous across social media and traditional media as well, showcasing this skulled figure with red eyes. He was terrifying and intimidating to behold. There was not one person in their right mind who would ever want to challenge him. Even if it were a matter of stopping an evil force.

#

Back in Japan, Tonya and Curtis were out to dinner at a Japanese Steak restaurant in the heart of Tokyo, Japan. On the TV at the bar, the Japanese restaurant went dead silent when they saw the videos and images captured of The Master.

Tonya and Curtis were both residents of New York City, where they had found a life after they had gotten married in Japan. They were both African American and in their mid-forties. They knew that something was up as they both had been celebrating a five-year wedding anniversary of when they had moved to Japan. There was a local contest that both had entered for the rights to a dojo school for men and woman. There were many contestants, but Tonya and Curtis had each studied under the best teachers, and being the newest faces, no one else knew much about them. They had each gone through the other contestants very smoothly, within their respective gender categories. No one was any match for them, and not one contestant gave either Tonya or Curtis a fight that was too difficult.

The prize amount was the equivalent of ten million dollars in Japanese yen. It was also under a veil of secrecy, in order to pass on the legacy for generations to come. There were many people who had seen this couple, one of whom was an old sensei that had been sitting and viewing these two individuals as being more dominating than any of the others. It was Tonya and Curtis, the married couple. The old man sat with a cane and looked like he could pass for a few hundred years old. He seemed to have more wrinkles on him than anyone on the planet.

The old man's name was Goro. He was short but muscular, and age didn't sit well with him. Goro sat at the table and watched very carefully, as most of the contestants that had entered the tournament were individuals he had taught. He had realized that the martial arts that Tonya and Curtis used was from around the Japan area. It was hard to see someone who wasn't a native of Japan gaining his treasured secret, and it was a large one at that. Still, most of the contestants knew that they were going to win.

Predictably, Tonya and Curtis received most of the secrets to the Triads, which was strictly confidential, and they were expected to keep the name going and the tradition, in which he had no blood descendant left. It was the way to keep the tradition going, and the way to protect the secret. They had gained the respect of each division from every man and woman, and before the night was over, they had earned the respect of the champion himself. He didn't stand well in his advancing years, so just seeing him in the arena was a huge surprise.

Tonya and Curtis were surprised, as they had won against what they had thought were much more advanced fighters then they were. There was a great intimidation factor that they had to face, and the crowd's jeers and booing against them did not help their confidence.

Goro invited them back to his home, up on the mountaintop in Tokyo, the next day. They were being honored, and Goro was dressed in a bright red outfit, which symbolized honor and respect. He had never invited any champions back to his house, which in Tokyo was more like a shrine of all the awards he had won worldwide.

The house was large and remarkable. It had shrines of paintings from different Japanese painters and various sculptures and other artwork throughout the house. Tonya and Curtis held hands as they walked into the living room. Goro walked slowly with his cane.

The young couple looked around and couldn't believe the house and how impressively decorated it was. Each room was something special. Next to Goro on a table was a long list that looked as if it was hundreds of years old, but had been preserved for that many years.

They both sat opposite Goro, who put on his reading glasses. Next to him on an old wooden end table was a book.

At his feet, the rug was also old, and many decorations appeared, too, as if they had been in the house since the 1800s. Goro, in his red robe, began to talk about the Triads and the history of the group. It was hard to understand how the young couple was given responsibility on taking control over this great group.

Goro spoke about the legends and the group that he had protected for generations, over many decades. His words slurred, making him difficult to understand.

Curtis was a tall and very broad man of 6'3" with triceps and intimidating biceps, and Tonya was very strong for her size at 5'7". Both of them were very attractive people as well.

Goro sliced blood onto the old paper from both their fingers, and with the sacred smoke that went up in the air, so did he. The times had changed, and it was the first time a Triad group would be run by two people who weren't Japanese.

It was unknown what the old ancient Goro next told Curtis and Tonya. Five years had passed, and all the things that transpired in the training facility were known only to them in all of Japan. The change was a difficult transition for everyone, but eventually, it brought on the new era. Curtis and Tonya worked hard, doing extensive training for both men and woman. They also changed the outfits to dark black cloaks with hoods on them. The married couple taught fighters to move gracefully from morning to night, and the many others around the world; with the technological capabilities, there was means of being alert to potential dangers.

Goro never got to tell them about The Master. He was one of only a few who had known about this legend. It was rarely spoken of after the downfall of Okla. Most had died with the knowledge, never breathing a word, and certainly not daring to let his name escape their lips after such dreadful events.

Tonya and Curtis were in the sushi bar to celebrate their five-year wedding anniversary. They could tell that seeing something on the TV from Tokyo and a lot of social media from New York, not to mention the dead silence in the restaurant, was a good indicator of what this person was and the severity of the situation. It was as if the whole city knew of him, and from what people had heard, it was a story that was said not to be talked about over the years, but it truly was. He had destroyed so much: that family of the Lees, and finally The Master leading and being frozen for 400 years.

Tonya watched and was interested as they both looked on. "Who is that?" she asked the waitress when she came over to the table.

The waitress wasn't surprised that they hadn't known, as it was a Japanese legend dating back 400 years. How would they know, as they were from America? She nicely explained to them both what had happened, and as she told it to them in an animated way, it seemed terrifying to them, and to others around them.

She handed the bill over, and they paid. She told them to go a few blocks, that there was a store owner who knew all about The Lees and The Master. "Go to him, he will let you know, and tell him that Kalin sent you," the half Japanese, half American girl said. "He comes in here twice a week. He has a lot of information. His name is Mr. Sasaki."

It was still early, and they both looked at each other. They had a responsibility to learn as much as they could about this monster. He was great and powerful, and as Kalin had described him, it was more important to learn about The Master than the average person. She seemingly knew a great deal more than most, and things just wasn't making sense. Something indicated to Tonya and Curtis that there was something about her that was not being said. Kalin looked like she was sixteen, but she was probably nineteen or so, but who truly knew?

Tonya and Curtis walked the few blocks between the restaurant, vowing to get to the bottom of this. Soon, they came upon what seemed like an old antique shop. It looked like it hadn't been open in years, maybe even centuries.

Curtis, with his big biceps, opened the door for his wife, as he always did. He looked at his wife, her great figure and beauty. He was happy to have her in his life.

"Let's go in," she smiled and said.

They walked in the store, which contained all sorts of Japanese treasures: books and things that could have looked hundreds and hundreds of years old. It was quite remarkable that the store hadn't been turned over a few times.

The lights were dimmed, and the shop didn't even appear to be open from the outside. That is why Curtis had been wary of turning the rusted door knob. It was a disaster from the looks of the outside of the shop, run down, rusted, and falling apart.

He really didn't want to go in, and neither did Tonya, as it did look a bit intimidating and creepy as well. There was more that they could have worried about as well.

The little old man stood as if he were one of the statues. When he spoke, it nearly gave them both a heart attack. "Come with me," he said.

Mr. Sasaki was a very old man with a robe and a small walking stick. He couldn't be more than five feet tall. He remained silent, as he walked and waved his hands towards them. They looked each other. Behind a bookcase was a deep tunnel down a long and windy staircase. He kept on waving his hands towards them. The staircase looked like it was hiding something. What kind of creepy old man trusted two people he had never met, they wondered?

The old man, Mr. Sasaki, walked and had lifted up his robe as he had walked down the winding staircase.

Tonya and Curtis walked with hesitation, but the old man called their names, and said "come on" with a very powerful but low-pitched voice. "You need to see these things," he added sternly.

They walked towards the staircase and noticed torches on the wall. The bookcase behind them closed solidly. As they walked down the staircase, it struck them that this wasn't a place for two people out for their anniversary, as Tonya was dressed in a pretty red and white dress, and Curtis wore a black suit and tie. This wasn't exactly the intended plan on their wedding anniversary to walk down a creepy staircase in an antique store. It was good for them, though, that both spoke Japanese. However, this man also spoke English, so that did help as well.

Curtis and Tonya descended into a room of treasures and things that had been discovered, and passed on to Mr. Sasaki. It was a room full of all things pertaining to the Lees and The Master. It had to be hundreds and hundreds of years old. The books, the dishes, the weapons, and everything from the bookcase to the other things that they couldn't imagine.

He took off the cloak that he wore, revealing a big gash along the side of his skin, from what could have been a sword fight from god knows how long ago. The torches were stationed around the stone walls, and they held torches to light the room. There was a book on a small wooden table. Mr. Sasaki didn't say much, but he knew a lot about the subject at hand.

He began to tell them all about The Lees, but first asked if they were sent to him by Kalin the Japanese waitress at Tokyo's Tuna Heaven. They answered and told him yes. He smiled, and he said, "She always said someone would come to me when I would eat there twice a week."

Mr. Sasaki opened the old book and showed them things that they didn't think existed, and neither did anyone else. But, then again, no one else knew what Mr. Sasaki had, and how these objects had been passed down from generation to generation, though he had never asked about how they were originally acquired. It was a "don't ask, don't tell" type of situation.

They spent what seemed like hours downstairs in the basement. He showed them everything, and explained the story of who The Master was. He knew so much, and shared detail after detail, event after event. It was almost as if he had been there.

Tonya saw the grace and the passion he possessed while telling the story and knew where Kalin had gotten that part from.

Tonya looked at him and asked, after he had told them everything, "Why did you tell us everything about The Master?"

The old man Mr. Sasaki answered, "You will need all the help you can get as the new Triad leaders in order to attempt to stop The Master." He gazed at them intently. "I'm not sure, but I believe the five scrolls of terror, which The Master held in high regard, were lost in the mountain battle. To my knowledge, they were never recovered. If not, it may have ended up in the Museum of Natural History in New York in the 1990s. But I'm not certain."

"Well, it's a lead," Curtis said and gave Mr. Sasaki a grateful look. The old man smiled, leaning onto his wooden cane.

"There is something that you will need to help catch The Master, if that can even happen." He bent down and looked at them both while picking up an urn. "It was said to be the same urn that contained Radagast from when he disappeared. It has been in my family for hundreds of years. They have kept it safe for all those years from everything or anyone, and no one has ever found it. It had to do with being in the right place at the right time, going back centuries and centuries of the family blood line that was passed down. We treasured it until the timing would be right."

Curtis and Tonya looked at each other, as they truly didn't understand what the Urn of Symboltos was supposed to do in order to help them get The Master. Even the wrinkled old man wasn't sure of its full mystical power or what it was supposed to do. Those details had been lost over the centuries, and it was just found by chance. They just knew that it had something to do with The Master, and instead of allowing it to disappear, his family had taken it and hidden it away from anyone who would think of taking it.

It was kept for so long, and it was protected until he had to dig it out after seeing what had happened in New York. Mr. Sasaki, when it was passed on to him, had been told of its importance and the conjecture of what it could do, though no one really knew what it was capable of or what it was used for.

As Mr. Sasaki handed it to the couple, the rotted metal looked more ancient than any artifact in a museum. But it was made strongly. The outside of it was tinged yellow and very worn, and one could see how it had been maintained over the years. It wasn't in the best shape, but it was more about what was inside the urn that was more important.

Radgast had been waiting from the ashes that were in the Urn of Symboltos, which was supposed to end the reign of The Master. But no one had truly known that Radagast had been locked inside the Urn of Symboltos for at least 400 years.

Mr. Sasaki handed the urn to Tonya and Curtis, who thanked him for the major history lesson. He led them up the hallway to the storefront. He pulled the switch to open the bookcase so that it opened to the storefront.

They both walked out and wrapped the urn within the folds of a cloth covering to conceal it. It was difficult to see, as it was night. The streets were empty, and Tonya and Curtis headed back to the secret hideout of where the Triads were hiding.

The hideout was hidden in a very remote location. It was dark out, and most of the city had been resting for the night. They had only gone a few blocks, when they heard a big bang, far away from the shop. They spun around, and Tonya took off her heels in order to run barefoot, with Curtis moving back towards where the bang had come from.

As they ran, it seemed like it had come from the shop that they had left. Though this was puzzling, nothing at this point seemed the way it was supposed to be. They were in a whole new world that they couldn't even begin to understand. It was a mystery pertaining to certain things that they were told, and right now, Curtis and Tonya had no idea what to expect.

As they arrived at where the shop had been, it had completely vanished, as if nothing had ever been there. It was bizarre, but nothing truly seemed to be what it had been. They stood, staring. How could this have happened? They shared the same thought: it was puzzling, but they couldn't begin to understand anything or why these things had happened.

Tonya grabbed her husband's hand, looked into his brown eyes, and said one word: "don't." He usually had all the answers, and in this case, there was none to explain the sudden disappearance of the building. Tonya looked at him. "We are in for many more surprises," she guessed.

Tonya and Curtis left the front of the building, breaking into an easy, natural run. They headed back to the Triad group, and set a plan to head to New York.

Chapter 6

The weeks had gone on for Captain Thomas, and he had a lot on his mind, coming home to an empty house for the last few months due to his wife dying of cancer. Captain Thomas had done his best to keep his mind occupied with work-related things, and there seemingly wasn't enough time to even think about it during the day. Captain Thomas had seen his wife battle breast cancer and eventually pass after only a few months. It had been almost a year ago, and was still quite difficult.

He came home to stillness and silence. The knowledge that his two boys, Matt and Jack Rider, had been so distant from each other made his heart even heavier. It was truly sad to see his relationships with the two boys whom he had saved from being murdered in an alleyway in Manhattan so many years ago now evolving and growing apart. How had they fallen so far from grace as they had grown up, he wondered? The Captain and his wife had adopted and raised them, but he often thought he hadn't done enough.

Things didn't used to be this way. At first, it was always Matt who would get the recognition, academic awards and athletic ability alike; he could do it all. It was a battle that Jack didn't think that he could win at any point of his life. It was something that had always provoked jealousy between the boys. Jack felt there was no wrong that Matt could do, while he just tried to aspire to be like his brother. He was never good enough, it seemed.

When Matt and Jack had been adopted, a young Captain Thomas and his wife Laura were just newlyweds who had been talking about building their family. When at such a young age the two boys had seen their parents murdered in front of them, the couple vowed to protect them always, so that they would avoid the same fate.

It was so sad how foster kids were treated in the system, no matter how good or bad their story was. There were plenty of stories, just never good ones regarding how they end up there either. It had been such a long process from the incident of their parents' death, to finally getting them adopted. It was not an easy process having to battle the legal system. Finding out the legal guardians and that their uncle was an abusive alcoholic and sex offender was just another unfortunate event. The Thomas's wanted to have the boys in a safe home and a good environment as well.

It was every parent's dream to protect their kids. But it wasn't ever something that was simple or easy. There is no book to tell you how to parent or how to make the tough decisions. There was no guidebook or script in hand that would tell you how to do everything perfectly, especially considering where Matt and Jack had come from. Seeing their mother and father gunned down in an alley, and their father taking a bullet for his wife, trying to save her. But it really didn't matter as they both been shot in that alley.

It was something that then-Sergeant Thomas had heard. He had been a few blocks from being off duty, and he ran as he saw the boys and pursued the perpetrators before they could hop a fence. Sergeant Thomas had shot them both and killed them, eliminating the villains who had killed the Riders' parents.

It had taken a lot of counseling to start the healing process. It was a large undertaking, and adding to the complexity of the situation was the fact that they were one of a few that were African American parents to two white kids. What they had done was to save their lives, which was nothing short of heroic.

It was so pathetic the Thomas's would have to hear the slander and derogatory statements from others about their situation. They were good, Christian people, well known in the community. That's all that mattered to them. The Thomas's knew who and what they were.

Laura, his wife, had always prayed for her husband, that he would come home each night, and never have to receive the knock or phone call that he had been killed protecting someone or trying to stop a crime. There were so many funerals that the Thomas's had gone to, and the city dealing with the September 11th crisis wasn't easy as well. It was a difficult time to deal with, and having to handle looters and all the other crimes surrounding that drastic event was extremely challenging.

The stress level brought on by something as horrible as the events on that day was even greater, knowing a few months before they had been dealing with the Riders. That was such a strain on the Thomas's in many ways, but it was more mental stress than anything else. It was the hardest thing for them to deal with. But the Thomas's had a great deal of mental fortitude, too, and they engaged in many conversations at the dinner table, problem-solving, and that was even before they had the boys in their home.

It was the way that they both handled things, and the way that they had both been raised. Now, Captain Thomas saw the pictures of his sons each night, and the one of his wife Laura, and he had broken down and cried each night as he had walked into their queen's house. It was very difficult to even think, let alone do his job.

For almost thirty-five years they had been married, and he remembered everything about his wife—the great things, and the small things, and the larger things about someone so wonderful that he had met and begun to love in his life. From the day he met her to the day of their first date. All of the memories came to him. There was always something special shared between spouses, a mutual understanding of feelings, a connection. It was not easy spending all those years with someone and then having that dear love wrenched from your life. Laura had been the backbone of the family. While then-Sergeant Thomas went to work, she was fighting for every hair and inch on the two boys. As he gazed at the photos left on the wooden bookcase by the door, he remembered.

It was a rainy night when he had walked in, and he had hung up his raincoat on the coat rack by the door. He had taken off his long boots so that he wouldn't get the carpet too wet. He looked around and saw the photos from her funeral that were laid and scattered around the house. Captain Thomas's house was in disarray, and rightfully so. He hated coming home, as the love for Laura was beyond love an ordinary someone has for his wife. It was quite difficult for him to process the emotions.

However, Captain Thomas had to manage somehow, as tomorrow was a new day. He was going to pick Matt from prison. Matt had been wrongfully set up, and the Italian mafia had put him in this predicament, as a result of Matt getting too close to things because of his position.

Matt was special, and his father knew and had warned him about that prior. But it was the justice that he wanted in order to protect the city from the crooks that overran New York City as well. Captain Thomas knew that in the twelve years of being there, Jack had only visited him twice, when he had turned thirty, and one other random time. It was long before then when things had become tense between them, growing from the existing jealousy Jack had toward Matt.

But, in Jack's response, he claimed he had never cared what happened to Matt, even when they were in high school. The truth was that even when Matt excelled, the more he had done well, the more anger had been incited. In a way, it was like he had turned his back on him in every way possible. Over the years in an upstate prison in Otisville, this only festered within Matt. You only get one brother or sister, and how could such frustration over his jealousy over the years prompt Jack to only visit him twice?

In a way, Matt had done everything to look out for his brother, even while in grade school, in high school, and even during later years. Jack was tired of Matt trying to be the bigger one, always trying to enforce himself. But Matt always seemed to detect the trouble that Jack would get himself into. Whether it was the wrong crowd, the wrong girl, or the random situations that he seemingly got himself into, and whether it was Matt always trying to help him, or his parents trying to get him out of something that he had done. Jack had an innate sense about it.

None of them quite understood it either. What could have prompted these things that had taken so much time to finally come out? It was more than that. It was protecting his brother and the name and reputation of his father, who had saved them from near death, not to mention simply knowing right from wrong. There was no clear reason for all the trouble that he had put everyone through. There was never any explanation for the many things that had occurred to the family that had raised him, nor the other ridiculous things he had done or attempted to do either.

#

Life was never as simple as it should have been with the boys. There were always distractions or a favorite in every family. No one could pinpoint it, even after the years of therapy Matt and Jack had after their parents had been shot in front of them. That was an event that would have traumatized anyone, and one that Captain Thomas and Laura had problems with as well. It was a constant battle with the hard times without enough good times for their family.

Over the years it had become an unwinnable battle with Jack. Something in which Matt, Captain Thomas, and

Laura invested much effort with no real result. The therapy just never worked with Jack. It was the way he way shaping the type of person he was going to be. He was predisposed to be one whom you would always feel needed worry and concern. They didn't like it, but it was the truth. They would all wonder each time that he came home from school what note he would have or what call he would get from school about a problem or altercation.

Through high school, Matt had met Sherry. Women was an area in which Jack had a severe lack. Matt and Sherry hit it off right away. Sherry had grown up in New York, but had gone to different schools, winding up at the same school in Queens. They both went to Bayside High School. That is where they met.

At first, Matt was cool, his usual persona, and didn't think that he really liked someone. He had kept a cool exterior, never letting out his true feelings. He was very calm when he talked to her in the halls and even when they had classes together. As time had gone on from their first date together, they quickly became inseparable. She had a good head on her shoulders at the age of sixteen when they met. It was a perfect situation for them both. Matt would walk her to class, and he would walk home with her. To look at them, any parent would have no qualms about the relationship, for either child.

As for Jack, that was a completely different story. You just never knew with him either. That was the scary part. What was Jack doing, and who was he with? his family would wonder. It was something that not one parent would want to think about—what kind of person was your other son becoming, and who was he with? From high school on, that was always the worry.

As time passed, the situation grew worse as well. That was something that the Thomas's couldn't really worry about either. The couple was able to pick up on those small things. The only problem was when you are raising small children, it's one thing, but as the age grows, so do the problems and the things that children get into trouble with.

As Matt and Jack grew up and made their way through their required schooling, it was always very evident which one was the more dominating over things like that. When Matt had met Sherry, it was like it was the perfect match, in many ways: similar families, similar lifestyles, and the same tastes on many levels. It was as if there couldn't be any wrong. It was like he was the perfect son, flawless in every way. WI school team, Bayside High School in Queens. Truly, he was a good all-around athlete, but he was also fantastic at everything he did.

Jack always seemed to be in Matt's shadow in every way. It just never seemed fair. It wasn't like Matt never attempted to help him with anything that he wasn't good at, in which he had more experience. Matt was the one who had always made time to do that, no matter how busy his schedule was, and in spite of being younger. He was a helpful kid on many levels.

That was another reason Sherry had liked him right away when they first met. His willingness to help others, and his humility drew him to her. Those defining characteristics were evident in his daily life.

Matt had done his training at the police academy, and even there, Sherry was by his side. Matt and Sherry's love had blossomed from being Prom King and Queen to then entering the police academy together.

It was something rare to see a bond like that. Captain Thomas would have loved to see his deceased wife get to see this from Matt's side. He saw each day growing up, and the years before Laura had gotten sick. It was the best feeling seeing one of the two boys doing well, and even though it was hard to not see Jack as well, he was still a success in other ways that didn't shape the way Matt was either. But, it was more about the whole family, the Riders and Captain Thomas, which was the hardest thing to see splinter apart.

Matt had taken it hard when Laura died, as he had been in prison knowing his mother was dying, and he couldn't see her truly before she had passed away. That was something that Matt had a lot of anger about, and when he had received that call, he had cried his eyes out in his cell, and Sherry had taken the drive up to see him the same day that had happened, to tell him.

Captain Thomas was so saddened, but Jack wouldn't even consider going with Sherry, as Jack just seemingly turned out to be a nasty person over the years. It wasn't like Jack never had those same chances or opportunities to do the same things in life that Matt had the chance to do. It was simply the fact that those opportunities that Matt had were those Jack never took the chance to do.

Matt had heard the news about his mother, who had pretty much saved him from near death. Jack, over the twelve-year span, had really never given much thought of ever seeing his brother again. His father wondered where his thinking was at all, or if he even cared about anyone or anything at that point.

The night before, Captain Thomas had been home, and had drifted to sleep on the living room floor while looking through the albums and old pictures from the funeral. He lamented how his son Matt wasn't able to come home because of his jail time for the last twelve years. Matt had been working a case that had spread over the local papers and national news about the Italian Mafia.

Matt's father knew how he was getting close, as everyone around Matt knew something was happening or they were getting injured. The more that Matt was digging about the Italian Mafia, the more people were getting hurt and injured. It was a predicament because they had set him up for a murder and sent him to the trial to judgement. It was everything that had worked against Matt in every way possible, and there was no way that they could defend Matt, as much as they had tried; it was seemingly a conundrum that wasn't going to end so well in the way that they needed it to.

Matt saw this coming, and Sherry had cried as their relationship was the hardest thing, but she had loved him from day one. He soon went to trial and was found guilty, as the Mafia had Matt out of their way, since he had been such a thorn in the Italian Mafia's side, and getting rid of him was the best thing that they could have done. It was the one blunder he had, and not finding his gun in a major shoot-out, not locating it until a few days later. By then, the Mafia had set the trap with evidence of Matt's prints on the gun of a killer. It was hard to even defend it, as all the Mafia members were all on the jury and had influence over the judge.

It was a combination of many wrongful pieces of evidence all pointing towards Matt. Finding a lawyer to represent him was impossible, as Jack had his moments and had caused even more belief that he had been just the brother that Matt never believed he had. He wasn't seen as that, and never had Matt's back during anything. He even went so far as to try to take Sherry from Matt, which was so wrong in so many ways. His own brother's girlfriend. How could one's own flesh and blood do something like that to one's own blood? It was an atrocity.

It wasn't easy for relatives of Matt and Jack, and they all sided with Matt, having seen what Captain Thomas had said to his family about Jack. Now they saw firsthand how Jack had become and the litany of problems with everything that he had done as well. It was so hard, as Matt tried to do everything right, and at the end of the day, Jack never stood for what was right. He totally turned his back on his family and friends as well.

The one that was hurt more was Matt, as he was being locked away for twelve years, which was clearly a very one-sided victory for the Mafia. It was a simple plea to the police department of New York to keep your nose clean and keep out of their business. It was a message that they controlled everything and anything that they could get their hands on as well. That was a truly scary and sobering thought.

After the trial, they said their goodbyes, and Sherry was there supporting her boyfriend, but Jack was nowhere to be found. It was a hard thing to accept, as the mental breakdowns and the anger that Matt had to now be alone had definitely thrown a wrench in his plans, as he really wanted to marry Sherry, and he even had a ring that he was going to give Sherry one day. But now this had all happened, and he'd have to spend time away from her.

Being led away from his sentencing day was the hardest thing—not to get to lie next to Sherry or even hold her hand. It quickly took its toll when he was locked in his holding cell waiting for his trial. That was the hardest thing, being away from Sherry. When you are in love with someone, not being with her on an everyday basis makes everything even harder.

He sat in his holding cell. Not seeing her, being alone, was excruciating. When he got sentenced, he knew that through the trial, even the lawyer team he had said that there was something more to this than he could put his finger on. It was hard to pinpoint but Matt had seen that he was clearly set up as well, and that had left a bad taste in his mouth. That was the one thing that he knew for certain, and it was difficult to understand why. But Matt knew as close as he had gotten to the Tianjin Mafia, there had to be something that they were truly hiding and didn't want anyone getting close to what Matt had gotten.

Matt's day came and went, and the kiss that had led Matt away would have to be one that would last and be remembered for the next twelve years. Matt, the muscular 6'0" tall cop, seemed to always be in great shape and always had the right turns of phrase. But he knew he was set up somehow. A lot of evidence didn't quite make sense, in addition to how they were able to do the things that they had pulled off.

When Matt heard the judge, the anger that he had was seemingly more on the side of the Mafia, meaning that they had a key card in their pocket and that was the one that had been used. It just seemed that it was a big thing, and they watched his car being taken away from Manhattan Court. It was all tears, as a lot of the city had been protesting and there was something that was seriously wrong with the way this all happened.

To the average intelligent person, it just hadn't make sense, especially not to any lawyer. If it smelled fishy, it usual was, and it was too dangerous to even let anyone dig. Matt was scared to let Sherry do anything, the way she had told him she would do. Sherry was much like him as well in that she never accepted the way the trial had gone and knew that something was not right. It was a result of Matt being too close to the Italian Mafia, and she suspected this as well.

The day had finally come after twelve long years, when Captain Thomas and Sherry were going up to the Otisville state prison where Matt had been kept in a cell. There were times that Captain Thomas and his wife had gone, and on other occasions, Sherry had driven Laura, before she had eventually passed away, just six months before Matt's release date.

It was hard, as Sherry showed up at the queen's house, now left empty except for Captain Thomas. Not seeing Matt's mother was difficult, and now Jack was gone too; no one heard any word from him, and he had only been up to see his brother twice in the twelve years that he had been in prison. It definitely showed his true motivations and revealed his character.

Sherry showed up on the doorsteps early enough to drive up to the state prison to be there to pick up Matt from his time being served. Twelve years had been a long time for someone to be locked up and to be removed from the outside world and society. His mother passing away and not being released to be at her wake or funeral and taken its toll, as had the absence of his brother. It made him think about a lot of things for the time that he had been away. The more he thought about it, the more upset he became. He had to make peace with certain things, but other events and situations just clouded his thoughts while he sat in a cell for twelve years. It was almost too much for him to bear, especially in isolation and with a lack of human contact. Soon, his time had come to an end, and he looked forward to rejoining society, and his family.

#

Captain Thomas and Sherry had left early in the morning to get Matt out at the designated release time of noon. Sherry drove, as she hadn't lived far from where Matt had grown up, and it was something that Sherry was glad to do. She had never dated another man or even thought about anything or anyone else.

That was the one thing that meant something. A twelve-year span of not being with anyone else showed how devoted Sherry was to him, just as Matt was to Sherry. She couldn't imagine herself with anyone else. Meanwhile, Matt slept in his cell all those years, often drifting off to sleep while wondering what things he had to watch his back over.

Matt had wanted to marry Sherry one day. He had felt that way from the first day he had met her, and every day after that as well. It was something where you just know from the way you feel about the love you have for someone. That truly never goes away from your life.

Sherry and Captain Thomas had gone up to the state prison, as the world had been changing and a new threat emerged. Sherry looked at the paper. The sexy redhead who stood 5'11" had pondered her conversation with Captain Thomas. Did he know anything about this new being who had instrumented the attack and broke out from the Central Park statue?

It was difficult to even know how to tell him that even had happened. It was a few hours that had taken them to get up there. The traffic was moderate, as New York always had that type of traffic.

After they had gotten out of the city, it was a nice smooth drive and a very rural drive, where they passed farmland, and the areas of farm that laid across the part of New York that some people do tend to forget about as well. Just like Long Island and some eastern borders of what some people tend to forget about New York. It was this scenic view as they headed east from the city. It was hard to know about resources from where you didn't live. That was a hard part as well: being in an unfamiliar place that was hard to get a good sense of. However, once they were past New York City, Sherry enjoyed looking out the window and seeing the land. A nice peaceful ride they had then.

Captain Thomas, meanwhile, had been reading the paper in the RAV4, while Sherry gazed out the window and wondered how peaceful things were going to continue to be after the arrival of this creature. Sherry over the last few weeks, along with countless others, never thought as him as any sort of peacekeeper either. In fact, he was quite the opposite. It was quite difficult to see him as anything more than someone ruthless and vicious.

#

It was noon when they had finally pulled up, and it was an overcast day like so many in New York. With such weather changes across the globe over the course of the last ten years, and the ever-evolving societal trends and climate, why wouldn't a change like this one happen in Manhattan of all places—a 400-year-old statue come to life. It seemed almost fitting to have happened here and nowhere else in the world.

What other place in the world could that type of statue and foreign warrior break out from the middle of Central Park. There were certainly creeps who walked around New York City, but being so literal about that was a bit much.

The guards prepared Matt for his departure, as it was nearing noon, and they had waited for him to change while retrieving his papers on his release and everything that his lawyer had requested. Captain Thomas had a lot of anger over the twelve years towards the warden and the entire state for not letting him attend his mother's funeral. That was the hardest thing to let go. It was hard to understand why, though they viewed him as a criminal. Just like everyone else and they really didn't care who he was or whose son he might be.

Sherry and Captain Thomas anxiously awaited his appearance. Finally, he walked out in the civilian clothes (a polo shirt and a pair of jeans) that Sherry had given to him the time that she had made it to visit him after Matt's mother had passed away. It was quite difficult to even hold in the emotion that swelled.

Matt, upon finally seeing his longtime girlfriend, hugged her fiercely and kissed her. Then he told her, "I've missed you till the end of the world." She smiled. She and Matt shared this feeling for each other, built on trust, love, and loyalty, which should always be the basis of what every relationship should be built on.

Twelve years living alone had been tough, and the one person that Sherry had loved had been set up by the Italian Mafia. She vowed that one day they would get what was coming to them somehow. Sherry cried as she held Matt. She never wanted to let go.

His father stood nearby, waiting for his moment. While he stood watching the couple embrace, he reflected on how difficult the time had been, Matt being away, many hours and miles away from New York City. He thought about the miles that each of them had put on their cars to visit Matt. There was no number of mile that either one would have hesitated to drive to reach him—their beloved son, and life partner, respectively.

Captain Thomas finally embraced his son, and the two men teared up. "Let's get you home," the father said, and the son nodded, emotion teeming in his eyes.

They walked out into the bright daylight. Matt had already heard from the newspapers, and the talk from the prison guards, about the strange warrior who had broken out from the statue. It was bizarre to hear about this, not something that you heard every day—that a 16th century guy emerged from a frozen statue in Central Park, prepared to wreak havoc. It wasn't something that had made everyday conversation, but since it was in the news so much lately, it had even gotten around to the inmates and became a conversation piece.

It was interesting to see the pictures of what he looked like; most would run the other way and not even think about it twice. How tough the other inmates thought they would be against this guy. The local and national papers still didn't really have a name or too much description about him. There wasn't any concrete history about it, despite that so many had tried to do research, but they couldn't fathom where to begin to find someone like him, from the 16th century. The fact that it was so difficult to find information made everyone believe that there must have been a reason for this scarcity, and probably not a good one, if attempts had been made to keep the details hidden.

On preparing for Matt's release, the guards fond a book that had been sent to him but never delivered. Matt was angry at the oversight and questioned why he had never received it. Either way, though, he had it now, and he took it along with his other belongings as he left.

Now he remembered the book and looked at it more closely. Where had it come from? It had mysterious wrapping, and the address was from Japan, from a Mr. Sasaki, the same one who had given Curtis and Tonya the Urn of Symboltos. He had no idea where it came from and what was in this strange brown book. It was very mysterious to Matt. Why would something from Japan be addressed to him? No one he knew lived there, and he knew Sherry had never been out of the country.

Matt didn't quite know what to make of it, nor did Captain Thomas. He couldn't pinpoint its origins. They also couldn't imagine how someone could have known his location. While they climbed into the car, Matt in the front seat and Captain Thomas in the back, the book tilted, and a letter fell out, falling between the two seats.

The Captain was in the back, as he was stretching his legs due to them being cramped after the many hours in the car. He got settled. The rest of his work documents were in the trunk. For now, he held onto the book, as if it had meant something to him. On the drive, he inspected its cover and flipped through a few pages, but he couldn't entirely focus. He was so ecstatic to be bringing his son home, finally.

Matt, on the other hand, now felt more confused than when he had been sentenced to go to prison, thinking about the book. Why would someone send it to him? Who was it? He worried that it was related to the Mafia. It just didn't make sense. Who was this Mr. Sasaki from the return address? He couldn't put the pieces together.

Finally, he noticed the letter lying on the floor of the car. He picked it up and read it:

What you will discover in this book will be of use to you when doing battle with great forces of legendary evil and revenge. Use this information wisely.

It was mind-blowing to Matt. He immediately snatched the book back from his father and began reading voraciously. He simultaneously commented on its contents, while he continued to rapidly scan the pages: he was one of those people that could read and talk at the same time while still maintaining his concentration. As he read, he noticed just from the look of the book, that every time he turned the page, it felt as if the book were going to turn to dust.

Sherry and Captain Thomas listened to the words, rapt. They all began talking at once, trying to untangle the meaning of the book and the letter. They wondered if this somehow connected to the unknown person who had attacked the city, the 16th century warrior. Could it truly be?

After a few hours, Matt finally came across something that captured his attention: a picture that closely resembled the one that had appeared on the front page of so many newspapers. It was a rough sketch, but still good and detailed enough to convey the details accurately. The picture was duplicated in a series that spanned the last few pages of the book, but no other information existed to indicate anything further, no text surrounding the images. The name of the artist meant nothing to them, but it would turn out to be a far descendant of a boy who had seen The Master destroy a shogun army, back in the 16th century.

In the text preceding the drawings was a brief description on everything that had happened in Okla and the centuries after, leading up to New York. Everything that had happened was truthful and accurate for all those years. It was just a book that had been passed on to be kept in the family name of Mr. Sasaki.

While Matt recounted these details, Captain Thomas had looked it up on his phone, and the more he had talked about it, the more information they could find about him. It was the big break that they had needed. It turned out that the long drive from the prison in upstate New York had afforded them the opportunity to focus deeply on the matter at hand, and it redirected their focus with a fresh perspective. This was something that Matt needed, from his particular standpoint.

They had been looking at the items at the end of this book that Mr. Sasaki had kept in his family for so many years. Matt researched the things as he read and talked about them during the drive; this kept the conversation going until they returned home. It was almost exclusively the only topic of conversation. How and why had this book ever been created, and how was it that he was able to get his hands on something so rare from Japan? Why was Matt chosen? But this would have, potentially, a significant impact on the way that this perpetrator of such heinous crimes was going to be caught. Looking at the picture in the book, and at the still picture that Captain Thomas had from the newspaper from a few weeks ago, it told a dire tale of what they were up against. There was no easy answer to an angry 400-year-old martial artist.

#

As they finally arrived home, Matt, Sherry, and Captain Thomas had all looked at each other, and compared notes once they had gotten to Sherry's apartment where she and Matt lived.

It was midafternoon. Matt continued to peruse the drawings and material in the back of the strange book, while Captain Thomas sifted through the notes and newspaper clipping from what they had on his name. While he sat in the living room, Matt reflected for the first time after walking into his apartment. Things still looked the same. Sherry had bought some new furniture to make the place look good for Matt, but she had arranged it the same way it had always been, and not much else was new or had changed. It felt like home, the home that Matt remembered, and it brought him great comfort to be in these familiar surroundings. This was much needed after being in that small cell for the past twelve years. He could finally breathe again.

The table was a beautiful fine wood finish, one of the pieces of the new decorative furniture that Sherry had arranged to have before Matt came home. It had been around fourteen years since Matt had stepped inside the apartment.

"The place looks amazing," Matt told Sherry. "I love everything you did with the furnishings."

"Thank you," she said, and leaned over to kiss him.

"It's even better than I remember," he said.

"And so are you," she countered with a sly grin.

As they all settled in, collecting their thoughts, they got their heads together. It was dusk and still the fall. They all gathered around the dining room table, the papers and notes scattered everywhere, containing any ideas they'd jotted down between the three of them—insights from Matt's book, their own conjectures, or other interesting pieces of research that could be useful.

They looked through their notes from the car ride, while Matt had been reading aloud from the book. They were struck by the fact that this unknown fighter's existence was cloaked in mystery. Where had he come from, and how had this all happened? So many passages in the book felt important, but upon further research, they hadn't amounted to much, but other things were simple to follow and dig up information about. The book that was sent was an enigma full of clues, some important, some not.

At this point, they had all worked up a bit of an appetite, as it had been a few hours that they'd all been in the car, not to mention that Sherry and Captain Thomas had an even longer trip from the ride up to the prison. Sherry decided to order food from a local Italian place that she and Matt had frequented while dating. It wasn't too far.

After Sherry ordered the food, they continued to brainstorm and each took a look at the back of the book. Matt sat between his father and girlfriend, showing them different things that he had found in the book.

He didn't know what to make of some of the things that he had read, and instead of sitting and relaxing around the house, he sat and dug into the book once again.

Soon, the time having passed quickly while they pored over the book, Sherry announced that the food had arrived. When she opened the door, the pure smell of the Italian neighborhood and all of its delectable food options wafted in.

They moved the papers around to the other side of the table, and pushed the things that they had written aside.

Matt inhaled the aroma again. It was the greatest smell that he could have smelled. It was so much better than eating the food at jail, not exactly gourmet food there. To finally have an eggplant hero was much better than the slop that they had put on his plate for the past twelve years. It was never the tastiest food, but he supposed it had kept him alive for the past twelve years. Still, he would never search for it in a restaurant; that would be unnatural to humankind.

He passed the book down to Sherry, and she looked at it again. She tried to find different things from what Matt had written down on the paper, and they both tried to see things from other angles that each one of them hadn't before. Even a name that they could find or something along these lines that would match up to some sort of modern person to help them find the individual. It was like the history of Japan had wanted to hide this person from the history books.

Captain Thomas and Sherry began to eat, as Matt finally ate his eggplant hero, which he had dreamed of while in prison, and now he could finally eat it again. Meanwhile, while he savored each bite, he looked at the back of the book again, to see if any of them had missed anything. Sure enough, as he glanced again, he saw a name written in very small print below the last image in the book. It read: The Master.

Chapter 7

It had been a few weeks since The Master had been heard from or even seen by anyone. The death toll was rising, though, and they were running out of body bags from the steady increase of fatalities each time that he had struck. Each night brought a new mystery of what tragic events would unfold with each new day.

The Master was in a big city now, not familiar with his environment. It wasn't the one of Okla mountain where he knew his surroundings so well. He had known only feudal Japan and fighting and training. He was in a place that he hadn't know or sought to know ever before. He had no place he had been staying for the past few weeks since his attack on Manhattan. He knew he had to find some type of shelter at some point to seek refuge.

He had jumped from rooftop to rooftop, and climbed up fire escapes. His quickness and jumping ability were far better than anyone else of his time or modern time alike. The Master was very old school, even as a 400-year-old warrior.

He was far better than anyone in the world, and much more dangerous than anyone else. That was the one thing that not one person in the world really knew—who he was or that he even existed, with the exception of the few who had known about him in Japan.

It was really a mystery even to the best people in New York who tried frantically to find out who The Master was and where he came from. The name they never had until Matt found it in the book that was sent to him. It was more a scrapbook of detailed things and events that had happened over the centuries and decades, but there was no author. It still was very odd. There wasn't much that could have been said to this point about who the police force was dealing with.

There was enough of a threat to have more patrols on the streets of Manhattan, and the safety of the citizens was a growing concern as well. There was so much that could have been considered. Such a vicious person as The Master was, and not one person would be able to keep up with him either.

Meanwhile, The Master went on his own time, and did what he had wanted when he wanted to as well. He saw that it started to rain one night and, leaping from building to building, this was enough. Being out in the rain when it did, and being in the mountains being taken care of by his mother were different.

He stood with his red eyes glowing in the dark at night. It wasn't the cold mountain of Okla. It was rainy and wet. But it was wet and cold and since it was the fall season, it was far from the weather of the cold and unbearable conditions of Okla mountain where he had grown up. The Master's lifestyle and training were still intact.

The city had no idea that he was as deadly as he was. You could go to any event that UFC was holding and it wouldn't have lasted that long. He was faster, fiercer, and more ruthless, not to mention that he had no pity or mercy for anyone that he fought. This was the same reason that dead bodies followed wherever he had gone. He never left people alive; he killed anyone in his path. There was no telling what he was capable of with so many people, and enough miles to use his swords, not one person able to put a stop to him. It wasn't as if he had to face any shoguns who would try to impede him. That's what made it difficult to mount an attack against him, too; there was no specific group of anyone that could possibly put a challenge to a warrior such as him, in any timeframe past or present.

It was nighttime, and The Master, like any swift warrior, always came out at night and rarely had any such daylight to fight. That wasn't his style in any way, shape, of form. He was very angry with those two swords that he had carried over the back of his armor. His lethal swings and the force of those swings were audible as the motions were so fast that the wind would talk as the swings reached the cutting point, so perfect in every way. There was no person, in New York anyway, who could have possibly stopped him; no one had the ability to do so. He was a killing machine, and with his martial arts and his fighting ability could kill with a variety of methods from the arsenal that he had.

He was just too dangerous to fight alone, as he had taken out so many of the gang members and police officers in the Central Park Massacre, as headlines called it. Not one cop or gang member out of the group of them could do damage to him.

They didn't know that 400 years ago, he had killed so many more than that single group of police and gang members on the mountain of Okla. If they couldn't stop him then, certainly no one in today's world could. He was almost more than human: a machine, and a fighter in every sense of that word.

There was nothing he couldn't do either. He spent a lot of his nights on top of buildings that had fire escapes, and he was never spotted; meanwhile, he hid during the day. Considering it was Manhattan, he had plenty of places to find concealment, but also being Manhattan made it quite difficult because so many people were around.

It wouldn't be hard to find a person like him, in theory. A red-eyed warrior with a clean silver skull, draped in heavy armor from head to toe. The two swords that were on his back, and the gear on his forearms as well. He never feared anything, and he continued his search for the scrolls, which he had looked for ever since losing them during the battle of Okla while coming down the mountain.

The night had been dark, and there was a feeling of foreboding and a brisk chill embracing the city, as if it were about to feel something much greater than anything it ever had before. The people felt the chill growing to the point of an eerie darkness. The sky's color was a mixture of dark blue and red clouds that had been very noticeable even from the New Yorkers. It had made them wonder about what the hell was going on, and for something to even worry New Yorkers was extremely hard to do, as most New Yorkers hadn't worried about anything or anyone as their default response. Some might have called most New Yorkers heartless at some point. But now there was enough of The Master to contend with, as he traversed the city, in search of his coveted five scrolls of terror that Orthor had created and lost during his domination on Okla mountain.

All of a sudden, a hefty laugh laced with evil filled the Manhattan skyline. An image of a black demon emerged, etched in the horizon. Most people who saw it were instantly terrified, and if those people hadn't been afraid of the times to come, then the threat was real.

Matt, Sherry, and Captain Thomas had all walked to the window from Sherry and Matt's apartment in Queens. They walked towards the window, as many people had, in a worried state, not truly understanding what was really going on, or who he was.

The police hadn't understood what was going on either. Matt looked at him from the window and gave a glance towards the others who were standing on each side of him. They had no ability to comprehend what was happening, as the demon with a robust, evil voice echoed a vibration that cut through the bitterness of cold and was felt more than what The Master was used to.

The demon spoke, and his words were listened to by all of the people of New York.

"An evil is coming, an evil that can't be stopped. Death to this city, and death to you all. The Master will make you beg for his mercy."

As Orthor spoke his name, a lot of people in Chinatown and other parts of Manhattan who were of Asian descent had known the story of The Master, but many truly never wanted to believe that it could be real. Now they had to confront this reality.

That was the one thing that instilled fear in everyone. It was as if you could hear a pin drop, and the facial expressions of the Asians were petrified, frozen. The pure image of Orthor, a demon that had come across the skyline of Manhattan, chilled them. The people of the city realized that their plague was so much more than they had imagined.

They were horrified at the new threat, on top of the existing massacres and reign of terror from The Master. Now they knew for certain that he was something from a different world. Worse, now there was a demon presence to contend with, too.

The pure evil laugh from Orthor was unsettling enough to make it unforgettable for all who heard it. The sound of the laugh: the pitch, the hollowness of that laugh, chilled them to the bone. He was an imposing figure to regard up in the sky, a black and monstrous demon. What in the world was going to happen to Manhattan now that The Master was here?

The Master saw the demon and remembered as he looked up, with a jolted memory from long ago, about him. He looked up at him, with a face that looked more like an enemy, as he wanted to rip his heart out more than help Orthor.

The Master never forgot that he took the skin off of his head, and that searing pain and memories that he never forgot nor ever forgave him for. Even after 400 years, he hadn't forgotten those painful things that he had done on top of Okla mountain.

His look was plain to see that he was not welcoming of Orthor's presence. The Master, at this point, couldn't defy who he was to an extent; however, his anger at seeing Orthor triggered an immediate feeling of outrage to the point where just seeing the image of him really made him angry. Anyone could understand how upset he would be just at the mere sight of him, someone who had taken the skin off of his skull in early childhood, making him into the monster he was.

The Master was on top of an apartment building, and the yell of anger that he echoed, carried throughout the entire city.

When the city's inhabitants heard it, most chose to lock their doors, to protect themselves. They knew what The Master was capable of, unlike most. Meanwhile, the police had been out all night, and Matt's brother Jack was on patrol. He never thought once to even call or see Matt since he had returned home. Jack heard the echo, along with everyone else.

The Master got off the top of the roof that he had stood on. He jumped down from the roof in a swift movement and looked around as he landed in the middle of the street filled with crowds of people. Being that it was New York, it was inevitable that no matter where he landed, he was going to be someplace around people. It wasn't hard to think about what he could do.

#

As Matt, Sherry, and Captain Thomas had all been on patrol together, the Captain gave the others numerous phone calls with orders, as the events unfolded. There was evidence to work with now, and Matt and Sherry, through their perseverance, had finally found information about him. Getting the name of the perpetrator was helped by the appearance of Orthor as well.

The more Matt and Sherry had found on him, the more things were finally coming together as well, completing the pieces of the puzzle. There was no help in sight, only the darkness of the night, and the darkness that had covered Manhattan was enough to evoke fear.

The Master walked down a busy 8th avenue in Manhattan, with the screams of fright pulsing around him after he had landed from one of the buildings he was on. He had made the jump from at least twenty-five stories up, and he managed not to break a leg or a single bone, but he did crack the sidewalk pretty well with the impact of his landing, destroying it.

The Master stood up, and the people who knew who he was scrambled from their cars, left there belongings, and ran for their lives. The Master stood on 8th avenue in Manhattan as if he owned the street. He stood tall, with the knowledge that his presence had the people running.

It wasn't hard for the police to find out where The Master was. Matt finally received a call from his brother—all about business and nothing else—about where The Master was. In Jack's voice, his hatred for Matt was still evident, as if he never wanted to hear his voice again.

The Master surveyed the fear of the people, and the police hadn't come quickly enough. A group of brave men and woman that had been training at a UFC gym came out en masse to help, and guide some people to safety, as the cars were trampled and city food stands and other structures were destroyed in the chaos. People continued to flee for their safety.

Thirty members had come out, seeing the commotion from the UFC gym. A clear path was made, and a 911 call came in from a reliable source, pointing them to where The Master was located. Captain Thomas, Matt, and Sherry received the call and headed to the area.

The cars were smashed from the left side of the street to the right side, totally demolished. The people were scared as hell, and all Hell broke loose as pandemonium had come to the streets of 8th avenue in Manhattan.

The people ran as fast as they could from the fearful sight of The Master walking towards them. His incredible, intimidating presence led to even more chaos as people fled. They had no idea what more acts of violence he was capable of. They didn't want to stand around to find out either.

He marched ahead, weaving in between the cars that had been trampled by the people running for their lives. The Master proceeded steadily, and walked as slow as possible towards the fighters who stood with weapons in their hands. The police hadn't arrived yet, and it was the people of the city taking a stand, trying to protect anyone they could.

The Master approached what seemed like thirty UFC fighters, both men and woman, from a local school that hadn't been too far from where they were on 8th Avenue. He had his bright red eyes, and his face was as evil to look at as the rest of The Master's appearance. His slow walk, his shape, and his facial expression were nothing more than a poised fighter. He wasn't the type to be challenged alone. Maybe with an army, and even that was a question.

It was going to be impossible to do anything with him standing right in front of everyone, as slowly as he had walked towards the UFC fighters who stood blocking the people who had run for their lives.

He surveyed his challengers, as they all stood with some type of weapon in their hands as well. He saw that they all had some type of instrument to use against him in a fight. UFC fighters had been trained to be the best fighters in the world. These fighters, though, didn't have a complete understanding of what type of person they were dealing with. This was no ordinary fighter, like they were used to facing.

He was so still, and he hadn't any reason to even reach for his swords at all. He never had reached for it, and the delay of this action was so evident. Meanwhile, all these fighters had lined up with their weapons in hand to defend themselves. The Master stood and kept his gaze trained on the people right in front of him. Now with purpose, he took steps towards them all. There had to be thirty or so men and woman, all wearing UFC gym shirts.

He walked a little faster, and a little faster still.

As the UFC fighters ran towards him, The Master jumped onto the crushed cars. He leaped into the oncoming UFC fighters, knocking them down as fast as they ran towards him.

The Master jumped up, and his speed was incredible. Being so close to him was a frightening sight, as the impact of his hands and feet stunned the fighters. The Master stood up and snapped the head of the first persons cleanly off, then stood up. The blood that gushed forth as soon as he snapped the head right off was unreal.

His power—his strength—was unreal. His stances were effective, as no matter how many guys charged him, the skill and technique that he had from each punch and kick, and the power behind each kick that he landed, was mind-blowing. The impact that each person received from his strikes was unbelievable.

There was no man or woman who wasn't scared to face off against him either. They were all afraid of him, and the way he had exhibited his skill, the way he threw around his lightning fast hands and feet in expert maneuvers, had them back on their heels. If they got hit, it happened faster than they all knew what hit them.

It hadn't mattered that there were thirty UFC fighters— even fifty would have not have made a difference at all, whether they charged The Master in numbers, or not. The Master would crush them individually or in groups; he cared not. No weapon was any use against him, despite their best efforts. They were outmatched. Each person was lucky if they could even raise their weapon before he had grabbed it and snapped it in half. He was quicker than any of them. Their muscles bulged from their UFC shirts, and they tried to use brute force, but this didn't work either. Whatever arsenal of fighting techniques they had was not enough. His level of fighting far surpassed any of them. To him, they were pathetic.

The New Yorkers tried to look back and could see the UFC fighters drop one by one, and in a very deadly fashion as well. It was something that was quite hard to even observe from a distance, as he had killed them all with his bare hands, and blood pooled around them everywhere.

Using his hands that were deadly as iron, he kicked and punched and used various other moves that were faster and harder than anything most would or could have felt. It didn't help either that standing in the gear that The Master did, his heavy armor, he would be impossible to hurt. How could anyone even attempt to hurt him with what he was wearing as protection? That was going to be impossible to even think to hurt him with the armor that he had on.

The Master swiftly went from cracking skulls to putting fists right through men and women's chests, ripping off arms, shattering skulls, breaking legs, and ripping legs and arms right off the different bodies of people. It was a bloody scene that would make anyone throw up from the sight of the horror and gore, and the quick work that he had made of some of the UFC fighters of New York.

As the yells and screams continued, he stepped over the scattered piles of dead bodies, and the body parts of each man and woman. He treated everyone the same and no one any differently. It was hard to imagine what would have happened if he had used a weapon.

Just then, The Master saw flashing sirens as he approached and stood over the pile of dead bodies. From the sound of it, the sirens were not too far from him. The Master didn't look twice but looked straight ahead from what he had seen. He had seen the approaching police cruisers and other vehicles, things he dreaded to see. But as Matt had pulled up with the Captain, Sherry, and Jack, there also seemed to be hundreds of police officers swarming around him, and they all had guns drawn on him. Meanwhile, The Master's gaze shifted.

The Master had seen something that drew his attention away from the nearing mob of police. What he had seen was a billboard that had images depicting the five of scrolls of terror on a giant display. This caught his eye immediately. He paid no mind to what was going on in front of him but looked past it to the billboard. He was more concerned about this picture of the scrolls. Matt followed his eyes and finally noticed it as well, but he might have been the only one who realized what the connection was to The Master and the scrolls.

Matt looked turned his head and looked more closely at what the billboard depicted. There was also Japanese language beneath the five scrolls of terror, which The Master was able to read as well. Matt saw the eyes of The Master, as he glanced down from the billboard. The Master saw Matt's eyes looking at him, too, and both of their eyes caught something from each other that neither of them would have expected.

The Master stood there breathing and realized that there was something about those scrolls that held some type of meaning to him as well. The Master didn't know where in the city he was nor where that museum was either. He frantically tried to understand the avenue and streets that would run parallel to one another, but this was hard to figure out even if you had lived in Manhattan.

The Master watched as Matt held his father's shoulder and pointed the warrior out to him, and they all had their guns drawn on The Master. Matt told his father to turn around and he showed him the billboard of the five scrolls of terror.

Captain Thomas looked to see the large billboard that had been on the side of 8th avenue. He saw what Matt had pointed out to him and remarked on his great observational skills. Those were the kind of things that Matt was known for. He was able to pick up on the little details that others might not have noticed.

As Jack looked on, even with all the noise, he was able to overhear what Matt had been saying to their father. As soon as they looked away and turned their attention to the billboard, they all saw what they had been talking about. Even Sherry easily saw what he been looking at.

The Master's piercing red eyes focused directly on Matt, and neither one of them had taken their eyes off of each other. Many members of the police force trained their guns towards The Master. He didn't seem to care too much about that. But it was the unbroken stare that a lot of people had noticed.

The Master seemingly didn't care about the guns, nor did he seem to realize what they were. The Master was immortal because of the power Orthor had given him from the five scrolls of terror. Though significant to The Master, it was something that no one else had really known, since it had happened nearly 400 years ago. No one was alive when it had happened and so much time had gone by.

Not one gun was fired at The Master, and now it was something that had become a major factor. Matt, Sherry, and Captain Thomas had realized that there was something about the scrolls that Matt had seen reflected in those red evil eyes of The Master. He was intensely focused on the scrolls, so there must be something about them.

The Master stood there in the street stained with the blood of his victims, which had dripped off of his body armor, and the things around the battle scene where The Master stood; the blood dripped from the cars, and the cement that the bodies had been laying on. The Master had gotten up and left, fleeing the scene as quickly as he had killed every one of the men and woman UFC fighters. This was just another mess that the city was going to have to clean up. It wasn't going to be easy, as the New York media would have to say something about it.

When Jack came over to approach Matt, the distaste for one another was easily read on both of their expressions. Matt was still very angry with Jack for having only visited him twice in the last twelve years. But Matt was possibly the best at figuring out things that seemed impossible, and Sherry shared this aptitude.

Matt and Sherry prepared to leave, as Captain Thomas and his other son both stayed behind to help with the cleanup efforts. He wanted Matt and Sherry to go back to the precinct where they all worked in Manhattan. Matt had told his father Captain Thomas that there was something about those scrolls, the book, and he was certain that Matt and Sherry, both working together, would somehow figure it out.

So, Captain Thomas had decided to give them the keys to his office.

"Here," he told Matt, handing him the key. "You'll need this. Your stuff has been sitting in the file cabinet with your badge and your uniform."

Matt gave his father a hug, and Sherry did as well.

#

Matt and Sherry walked away and took Sherry's red Rav4, driving off towards the precinct. It was only about a ten-minute car ride. As they parked the car, they noticed the precinct was empty, as most on-call units and officers around the city had been looking for The Master.

Matt and Sherry walked into the precinct, and both of them sat in the office where she had stored a few resources, including a few books on feudal Japan.

Matt had said to her that The Master would not be in any book in which they could even look up his name. But Matt had never been very tech savvy, whereas Sherry was well versed in both technology and books. They were great as a team. They worked well together and had a great deal of mutual respect.

As Matt looked on, he watched Sherry navigate the computer and find something on the five scrolls of terror. They both knew it had been sitting in the museum of Natural History since the 1980s or maybe even earlier.

Sherry pulled up a few different links on the computer. She read each one of them but they never had a person linked on any page who had found or discovered the scrolls. How was this even possible that with such an important discovery of the scrolls, not one person wanted to put their name on it? This made for a very curious question to which there was no apparent answer. How could anyone really want to do that? For now, the larger concern was about discovering what made The Master so fixated on getting his hands on those scrolls. Something about them had some type of unparalleled value to him. They wondered what it could mean.

Sherry had some information on the links she'd been scanning, and she found one that had a more descriptive story about who and what The Master was. She clicked on the link and began to read the whole story, and finally began to learn how the scrolls fit in to the larger story of The Master, then the details about the statue, and finally, the pieces that described how he had come to be the way he was today. She learned about his origins and where he ended up.

As she continued to read, engrossed, she conveyed what she was learning through a strong reaction—her eyes grew wide, and her breathing quickened. The slightly distorted image of The Master at the bottom of the page only reinforced her fear. Indeed, what she was reading confirmed their suspicions and added a layer of complexity surrounding who he was. Sherry gripped Matt's hand. He lowered his eyes, having been reading over her shoulder. They shared a glance. Things were as bad as they had imagined, and even worse than they had feared.

Chapter 8

Matt and Sherry had been at the precinct and were still the only ones there at the police station. She and Matt got up, and then they got his uniform unlocked from the office. His gun was in the same drawer.

They had been in the back where she had the key to a lot of the guns that had been taken away from criminals over the years. She was going through them now, as Matt had walked out to where the offices and the front desk were.

Matt stood, looking at two cloaked figures who had suddenly emerged and were standing near the front of the precinct. Sherry came to join him a few seconds later and stopped short at the sight of the two strangers.

Matt and Sherry looked at one another in disbelief, not knowing what to do next or what to think.

Matt continued to regard the two in the cloaks with suspicion. He finally asked, "Can I help you?"

The two figures took their hoods, off, and now Matt and Sherry could see that they were just an ordinary couple.

"I'm Tonya," the woman spoke, "and this is my husband Curtis. We're sorry to intrude like this. I noticed that you have some things about The Master on your computer browser there."

"Who are you?" Matt asked, still suspicious, as he'd never heard of anyone named Tonya or Curtis. "What do you know about The Master? What are you doing here?" he asked in an accusatory manner. He stepped forward to block the computer screen.

"Let me explain," said Curtis. "Have you heard of the Triads?" He went on to speak at length about their background and what had led them to the precinct under these peculiar circumstances. As they spoke about the bizarre events that had unfolded in their recent past, Matt and Sherry relaxed and were put at ease. They realized that they could be trusted, and moreover, that perhaps they could be of some help to them in their current predicament.

The two couples retreated into Captain Thomas's office, and Matt and Sherry listened as they essentially received a history lesson, as Curtis and Tonya told them everything they knew and had recently learned.

In exchange, Matt and Sherry told them about the things that they had found on the internet. As Matt began to tell them about the scrolls, Curtis and Tonya told them that they had just learned about the scrolls a few hours ago as well. They explained how they had traveled from Japan and told them they were the leaders of the Triads.

Matt and Sherry looked at each other with an expression of disbelief.

"We thought that group died so many years ago," Matt said.

Curtis nodded his head in understanding. "It's far from the truth," he said. "They are still around, and in fact, I'm the new leader, along with my wife Tonya here." He proceeded to tell them both how it had happened and why they were chosen.

The story convinced Matt and Sherry that each of them was there to put an end to The Master's vicious attacks, and collectively, they had to do something to stop him.

As they sat in the office, Matt and Sherry began to talk in more detail about the things that they had seen. Most notable were the eyes of The Master glancing at the scrolls.

"What do you think that could mean?" Matt asked Curtis.

The light-skinned black woman, Tonya, answered them both decisively. "It obviously has meaning to him. We aren't sure what exactly, but we did find out a little bit about it before we left Japan to come to New York."

They both talked about the look that Matt had seen on The Master's face as he looked up at the billboard where he saw the five scrolls of terror on display. It was something that Curtis and Tonya had only learned about from the girl at the restaurant where they had gone back to for their five-year wedding anniversary.

The waitress, Kalin, had told them all about the five scrolls of terror. Before that, the old man never made it to tell them about that, and that was a big piece of information to withhold, from someone who was sworn to stop The Master at any cost. The Master had been and still was a bad guy. There was no doubt about that. He was one who couldn't be stopped by anyone or anything, or so it seemed. The scrolls, the girl had told them, was very significant to The Master. Curtis and Tonya mentioned Orthor and elaborated about the creation of The Master's powers and the removal of the skin that had happened to him.

Both Matt and Sherry informed Tonya and Curtis about the terrifying demon creature that had come over the sky not too long ago.

Tonya looked at Curtis and shared a glance—they knew that this was something that could only lead to more destruction and death, which left very little hope for the situation that plagued the city. The knowledge was sobering and instilled dread in them all. The Master was known as a sought-out enemy from Manhattan.

"What the hell is so important about the scrolls?" Curtis asked. The little he had found out about the scrolls was not enough; there was still much left that he did not know about those magic scrolls and what they could do.

Matt decided to call Captain Thomas. He filled in his father about who Curtis and Tonya were and why they were here as well. Captain Thomas listened carefully to the debrief, but what seemingly caught his attention most was about the scrolls and how Curtis was the new tribe leader of the Triads, the old and ancient group that swore to protect.

"Protect what?" Captain Thomas asked to clarify what Matt had said, a hint of uncertainty in his tone.

Matt told him that he believed the couple, and that they had verified the truth on the internet. Matt and Sherry, after talking with both of them, had discreetly looked up the information to make sure that everything they had told Captain Thomas was real.

They sat in the office for a little bit longer, rehashing the things that they had talked about. Sherry had looked up everything to make sure that the new Triad leaders really were who they said they were. It was all true. Captain Thomas was the type to always have a small bit of doubt, but his distrust would be easily dismissed in this case.

Matt assured Captain Thomas over the phone that he and Sherry had double checked everything and there was no reason to question Curtis and Tonya.

Captain Thomas was always wary by default. Matt had a better sense of that, and at times it had bitten him in the leg, too. But, as Matt then hung up the phone with Captain Thomas, he knew that there was something more to those scrolls than he had originally felt. It was just one of the questions he had wondered about, of all the things that remained unknown. Matt vowed that he would soon figure it out.

Tonya and Curtis, sitting close to Matt in the precinct, observed how he had looked puzzled, and even to them, it was apparent that he was working through this problem-solving challenge in his mind. They could tell that he was one who always liked figuring things out, and even being just out of jail, he was already back to the same old Matt, focused on getting some kind of self-satisfaction in whatever way he could.

Matt had a feeling that something worse was still to come about those scrolls, and they would prove to be much more important than what they were led to believe at first. What it was, Matt didn't really know yet, but he would find out in time.

Curtis looked around with his wife, and he began to tell him something mystical could be involved in the mystery of those scrolls. He had brought with him the bag that was given to him by Mr. Sasaki. Tonya lifted the bag up onto the messy desk.

Tonya, the very beautiful black woman, unzipped the bag. She hesitated, as she wanted to make sure that showing them something like this was appropriate and that they could trust Matt and Sherry as well. Tonya proceeded to take the Urn of Symboltos out of the bag.

Matt and Sherry looked at it, puzzled as to what it could mean.

Curtis tried to explain what he thought it was, but like he said, it was given to him by the Japanese guy Mr. Sasaki. The old man had really never told Curtis or Tonya about what the powers were, if they even had any at all. All Mr. Sasaki had said was that it had been in his family for decades, but he didn't mention any more specifics about its power or importance.

Curtis and Tonya had no idea what it was or how it was going to affect their situation. Matt looked at Sherry as Tonya had uncovered the urn and left the rusted and beat up object on a police officer's desks.

Sherry finally asked, "What does this urn have to do with anything that we are trying to figure out?"

Tonya and Curtis really had no answer for them. They didn't know how this old-looking urn would have anything to do with The Master, but neither one of the couples would be surprised at anything that would have come up at that point. Somehow, a suspicion told them that perhaps this strange object would indeed become useful in some way.

#

It had been a few hours since the two couples had met, and the four of them had been tirelessly trying to figure out The Master's next move. The body count had continued to increase, too.

Jack strode into the precinct just then, having walked away from helping his father Captain Thomas. Captain Thomas was left cleaning up the UFC bodies with the other police officers on 8th Avenue. Jack had a very explosive personality and really didn't care about others, only himself. It was one of the reasons why Matt and Jack had always butted heads, from school, up to this current time as well. There was no clear identification as to why, and his motivations were not born out of anything that Matt had ever done. It seemed more like it was derived from the way Jack had felt about Matt and his own nature.

The more Sherry had interacted with Jack, the more the red-headed girlfriend of Matt's had developed a strong distaste for him. Sherry had witnessed his behavior, and now, even Curtis and Tonya were picking up on the tension and the dynamic between the brothers and between Jack and Sherry. They could judge for themselves all the same; the way he swaggered into the precinct told them everything they needed to know.

Jack had pushed the two double doors open. He immediately started screaming at Matt. He looked at Matt as if he were going to try to kill him.

Tonya shot a look at Matt, then turned to Sherry. "Angry brother, I see?" she said with a raised eyebrow.

Sherry grinned. "You really don't know the half of it," she responded.

Matt looked at his brother and glared. "This isn't the time nor the place," he said. His emotions bubbled to the surface.

Jack glowered and charged toward him, still yelling.

The pair went forehead to forehead with the anger towards one another. As they finally let it go and unleashed their frustrations, face to face with one another, they looked like they were about to come to blows with each other.

The Master had been watching the eruption of sibling rivalry from the rooftop. As evil and supernatural of a being as he might have been, he still was human at his core and could pick up on those things that were inherent in human interactions. As The Master watched from the wet rooftop of the precinct, he observed the scene long enough to know what was going on.

The Master stood up, finally having seen enough from his perch high above. There was a long enough pause to allow The Master to prepare his next move. His eye caught on the glass pane on top of the precinct's roof. In one swift motion, he jumped right through it, and the glass came crashing down from the roof.

All of them inside immediately recognized who it was. They all ran and scattered in order to avoid getting hurt from the glass that was right beneath them all. The Master landed on a desk, and the weight of him went right through the desk on impact.

Curtis and Tonya lunged behind one of the many desks to get out of the way. Matt and Sherry followed suit. The Master stood in the main room with the desks, chairs, phones, and papers scattered all around him in disarray. He stood in the center of the chaos.

The large samurai warrior with his swords and red eyes blazing in a thick skull regarded them with an evil stare. He had swiftly surveyed the room to see the police precinct in shambles. With the contents of the desk scattered all over the place, the doors busted open, and glass littered everywhere, it was a mess.

Tonya and Curtis had guns, and they quickly drew them and started to fire at him. The Master stood there defiantly, and the bullets bounced off of him.

Curtis and Tonya were in complete shock, as were the rest of them. They froze in disbelief.

The Master smiled in response to their terrified expressions, then he lunged for Curtis and his wife. As he tried to protect her, Curtis was grabbed by the fierce warrior, and the punches and kicks that Curtis was landing had no effect on him, let alone the gun, which had no effect, especially after The Master seized and crushed it with his bare hand.

He took Curtis and launched him through walls, crashing through the glass of Captain Thomas's desk, splintering it apart. Curtis lay motionless in the wreckage, all bloodied up from what The Master had done.

Tonya and Sherry tried running away as The Master launched a computer chair. Tonya flipped over a desk and got knocked out from the impact, her prostrate form sprawled in the middle of the precinct's floor. Sherry quickly scrambled away.

Matt charged up to The Master next, and he easily grabbed Matt and catapulted him out of the precinct entirely, sending him out to the street.

Jack was left by himself to fight The Master. He was cornered all alone, and he had no idea where to go, nor did he have anything to use to defend himself either.

The Master stood 6'3" with his shiny warrior's skull, and gleaming red eyes. He stared at Jack, conveying all of his evil intentions without having to speak a word.

Jack, however, never knew when to give up, even when faced with insurmountable odds. So, he stood tall and spit in the face of The Master. This was a most unwise action.

As he spit, The Master looked at him with disgust and wiped it off of his face with a sneer. Now The Master was furious. Jack had nowhere to go, and no one to save him either. He couldn't move, and no matter which way he tried to escape, The Master wasn't going to let him.

Jack took a swing at The Master and caught him in the midsection. The Master merely smiled, as the punch didn't seem to faze him too much.

The Master continued to grin, and grasped both of his hands together with the shapes of fists. The Master with such great force struck Jack with a single punch that knocked him down to the floor. The strike was extremely hard, just like all of his moves were, and it was painful, too. The Master followed up with another hit, and then another, each time Jack tried to stand up.

The Master went to work, rapidly bashing his face in with multiple punches, causing Jack to bleed more and more from each punch.

While The Master was occupied, Sherry emerged from the place where she'd been hiding, lying under one of the desks, which The Master had flipped over. He hadn't seen where she had gone. Hurriedly, she had scattered around on the floor looking for the urn so that she didn't get spotted by The Master as well.

After a bit of searching and crawling, she spotted the bag, and as she did so, The Master was beating someone, but she hadn't seen who it was, as things were happening so fast.

Sherry grabbed the bag with the urn in it, and fled from the building as quickly as possible. The Master caught sight of her out of the corner of his eye, as he tossed Jack into the middle of the room. The Master looked at Jack. Every part of the man's body was sore, and he had suffered blows on every available inch of his body.

The Master walked slowly over to him, looking down upon him, and saw a body that was still moving. As Jack tried to move, as slowly as possible, The Master looked on. The man had to use great effort just to crawl a few inches.

The Master took out one of his swords. Meanwhile, Jack used whatever strength he had left to move, and he placed his right hand on the floor, where a lot of his blood was in various places—whether it was from the glass or the blood that he had lost from The Master was anyone's guess.

The Master watched Jack put his hands down, and his right hand was on the ground. The Master had his sword in his own hand. He took it and put it right through Jack's right hand. The sword pierced right through the floor.

Jack screamed in agony, and his face contorted, as the tears of pain ran down his face. The experience was an unimaginable kind of torture. Besides the sheer pain, the amount of blood he had lost was staggering, and he didn't know how much longer he could last.

The Master circled Jack as he writhed on the floor, and he saw that he was just about dead from the punishment and the growing pool of blood where he lay. The Master shot a parting glance at him, then simply walked away, heading straight out of the precinct, not knowing where the rest of them were. The Master was quickly out the door, and then he was gone.

Matt slowly tried to move and stumbled as he attempted to get back onto his feet. He had landed extremely hard and was stunned, leaving him staggering, but eventually he regained his footing.

Sherry had got back into the precinct and yelled at the top of her lungs for Matt. Matt responded.

Curtis and Tonya both lay on the floor, having been knocked out from the impact of having been tossed as well. As they finally came to, little by little, they tried to recover. They heard the sounds of breaking glass and destruction— not the best way to have woken up.

Tonya's arm hung limply; she had a busted shoulder, after being thrown through the wall. Curtis, meanwhile, was dragging his leg as he called Tonya's name. He could barely move at all. His leg was broken, a bone dislocated. He couldn't even turn his head at all either. His face was twisted in agony, and his foot was turned the opposite way. The only thing matching his facial expressions of pain was the devastation of the precinct's damage.

Matt finally got up outside the police building, and he had heard Sherry's cries for her boyfriend. As Matt came hobbling inside the police building, he saw Jack all bloodied and mangled, as his brother lay in a pool of blood from head to toe.

Matt wiped away the sweat and blood that he had been covered in while flying out the window by The Master's hand. He called 911, and within minutes they had arrived, as there were plenty of hospitals around, and there was one around the corner from where they were as well. While Matt waited, they all looked at each other and at their surroundings. Matt had a limp from how hard he was thrown.

Tonya was lying still now, as she was calling for someone to help Curtis, who was in agony. Captain Thomas was notified of the event that had happened as well. The heavyset man ran as fast as he could, even though he was very winded after he had run to them.

He saw how bad Jack looked, and Captain Thomas immediately grabbed onto both of his sons' hands. "Get this guy," he said fiercely to Matt who looked into the eyes of his father.

Jack was swiftly attended to, when the ambulance arrived, by the EMS responders. They acted fast, seeing the state he was in. It was clear to everyone, both the emergency responders and Captain Thomas, that without fast action, the consequences could be dire. Captain Thomas cursed under his breath, wracked with anxiety and heightened emotion for his son.

Matt cast a glance toward the EMTs as they loaded his brother Jack into the ambulance. Meanwhile, Matt was busy, about to put Curtis's leg back into place. Curtis had a cloth in his mouth, as the way Matt was going to twist his leg and snap it back in place would be excruciating, to say the least.

Tonya lay with him, as Matt held his leg, and Sherry watched as the ambulance had pulled away from the building. Sherry was upset, as they all were, about the critical nature of Jack's status, bloody, on the verge of a fatality.

Matt saw them drive off, and as he did, he twisted the leg of Curtis back in place.

Curtis had bitten down really hard on the cloth that Tonya held, his head propped on her legs. The tears of agony and pain came pouring down his cheeks and soaked the cloth. Matt did what he had to do in order to help him. As he did, he made a sharp crack that had put everything back into alignment with his leg.

While Tonya stayed kneeling over Curtis, Matt stood up and walked away from the scene, watching the lights of the ambulance go on and flash as they sped away from everything. He tilted his head toward the destroyed office—the entire precinct looked as if it had been looted a few times over.

The Master was gone, Matt's brother was being taken to the hospital, and a whole load of dead bodies were all in body bags across Manhattan as well. The ordeal that had been so long and ongoing provoked such anger in Matt, and he had only been back a few weeks now. As the time had gone by, it seemed as if it was forever, but there had been enough anger over many of the other things that had built up over time. What was going to be the end game, he wondered?

The Master, for his part, was far from done, and there was going to be more Hell to pay.

Tonya was trying to help Curtis walk, and now they saw that the Triads had come, as they saw their leader was in pain, and that The Master had struck. As the Triad leader walked by himself, he looked wounded, and what seemed like a fleet of fifty or more approached; the group looked like something straight out of a movie. It would become useful to a certain extent, since bodies had been dropping and dead people were left all over the city. It was time, as the police force was battered and wounded and there was not one safe place left to go.

Chapter 9

The Master had been gone, and it was time, as he was on the lookout of where the scrolls had been. There was something about the scrolls that held meaning for him. The Master had wanted them back. Since he had been in a city and an unfamiliar place he wasn't entirely certain where the scrolls were either. He had no idea where to begin to search. He had realized how the city streets of Manhattan had run, and that alone was a feat even for some people to figure out. The Master, after a few weeks, had thought that he had, and it was mostly just guessing at this point, but the more he learned, the more confused he felt.

He kept remembering the street and the avenue. He remembered that, but just getting there was a maze by himself. He had been traveling all over, from North to South to East to West. It had seemed impossible, as he had spent weeks trying to find it, since his last encounter with Matt. He had little remorse about that.

There was something about The Master that was very focused on finding the scrolls. Orthor had given them to his parents and granted their power to The Master, making him immortal. It went back to his training in Japan 400 years ago. The Master was a truly different and unique entity, and there wasn't one person who was capable of stopping him.

Gaining the power of immortality from Orthor wasn't something that was handed down so easily from the demon that had been locked away for such a long time. As he had seen something great within him, and as his greatness seemed to be limitless, Orthor had believed and had great faith in him. He had seen his abilities with his two eyes. At some point, Orthor wanted him to be part of the six dark horses, his rulers of the world that he could govern. That was the type of potential he saw residing within The Master. He saw something much greater than mortals, and he was well aware that this warrior was special. That was his impetus for having created the five scrolls of terror, giving The Master immortality so many years ago.

The Master had spent what seemed like forever going all different directions, traversing the city and still not finding where he needed to go. The police department was on high alert for any sightings of The Master, and they had issued a city-wide warning about what was going on in order to alert the public and its citizens as well. There wasn't one group of individuals who hadn't been warned via radio, TV, or social media. Word spread quickly.

The Master grew agitated with everything and with not being able to find what he sought. The Master was strong-willed. He eventually caught sight of signs that he had followed, and he looked at them. He didn't speak English or any language that was current. He spoke an old unfamiliar language that hadn't been spoken in hundreds of years. It wasn't as if he could go and ask anyone either, especially with his reputation. He was the last of a dying breed in Japan. He was something different, something more devasting then anyone in the history of the country had ever known, besides his mother and father, of course. But he was the one who had been feared more than his own parents. He had been feared much more than any other leader over the years.

The Master continued his quest, gradually seeing more signs and advertisements for the Museum of Natural History. He had realized he was following the signs throughout the streets and the signs that were up from the buildings that he had seen scattered around the different places in the city nearby.

There was high security implemented all around, as the museum and the different blocks and streets were well patrolled. Captain Thomas had been back and forth between the hospital to see Jack and to take The Master down as well. There was now only one real way that they had figured out to take him down.

Curtis and Tonya had remembered something about the urn, but it still hadn't made sense regarding when the time would be right for the urn to be useful. Truly, the Urn of Symboltos was a mysterious object. They hoped they would know the moment when it arrived and be able to employ the strange urn in a way that would prove effective.

Captain Thomas was angry, and the city was on lockdown, while a wounded but walking Curtis, the strong African

American, despite his strength was looking extremely weak from the way he had walked. It was hard for him to have weight on the leg since Matt had popped it back in his socket. Captain Thomas had known that things were getting serious, as he had ordered police patrol more towards the Museum of Natural History than in other areas.

For their part, Tonya and Curtis had told the fifty Triads to keep watch of the museum, and the order by the police force of the city was something even greater.

It was dark and cold out, and The Master wasn't far from where the museum was on Central Park West and 79th Street in Manhattan. The blue and red lights filled the city, and the showdown of the police department and the cops was more than enough to instill fear in the city's inhabitants. It seemed as though they were on high alert.

The Triad group had been all around the city, covering the tops of each city building and trying to think of where The Master could be as well. There were no clear signs of him from what they could find, despite that there had been so many of them searching, and they had all been in groups together.

Curtis was still very hurt, and Matt and Sherry had been in the car patrolling as Captain Thomas had Curtis with him in his car. Matt kept an eye out, along with Sherry, as they knew he was an extremely dangerous enemy to face, from firsthand experience.

The streets of Manhattan were quiet and deserted, something that the people of New York weren't used to at any point in its prior history.

The Master, meanwhile, had been watching from the various points of the city, as he was nearing closer and closer to the museum. He knew that something was afoot, and it was something that only empowered his feelings about who he was. He was a strong warrior who was far above everything and anything.

The streets were empty, so that the citizens of New York would be safe—a city on lockdown. No way of going over bridges or tunnels, as they had been barricaded from both sides. There were so many things that they had to think of, how to protect the things that they needed to protect most. The Master, as he was lurking and watching their every move, found it very interesting as they had moved so swiftly about everything that they had to organize in order to control just one person in a city of millions.

In a matter of a few weeks since Halloween, he had killed so many during a short period of time. It was the perfect way for The Master to reign his terror on a city, just like he had done in Japan 400 years ago. There had been not one person in the history of the United States who had killed more by himself. He had terrified so many of the people in Japan and now in New York. His killing spree was more than anyone could have ever achieved; it was unthinkable.

The city streets appeared like a war zone and not one person or building hadn't been affected by it. The city was deserted, left empty as if the population had suddenly vanished, leaving behind papers and garbage, and fires from all of the looting. It was hard to see the city like that. For those who dared to peer out their windows, it brought a lump in their throat and a tear to their eye, both in sadness at the desolate sight and fear of what was to come. There hadn't been anything that Manhattan could have compared this to either. Not one specific period of time in its history had been such a deadly time.

The Triads had seen the advertisements of the scrolls. Some of them were drawn to what The Master had been looking for as well. There had been so much that they could do with the scrolls. The Triads saw all the signs that The Master had seen from one side of the city to the other as well.

The Master hadn't ever heard of the Triads and never knew of their existence. He continued to watch carefully and saw them move quickly. The Master was kept hidden in darkness, and not ever seen, no matter what part of the city he was hiding in.

It was evident that The Master had been ready for something significant. The Triad group scattered across the city of Manhattan but really couldn't find the evidence that he was still around. It was like The Master was a ghost. With so many looking for him, how could one person in such a small block radius disappear? There wasn't any sign of him.

Matt had been with Sherry and kept the communication open on the radios that they had all had, as they diligently continued to patrol the city in search of The Master. What was it going to take in order to find him? Hopefully the red-eyed martial artist wouldn't kill anyone else in the meantime.

The Master hadn't been too far from the museum, as the flashing lights had been a simple way of indicating his destination. The warrior came out with his two swords and stood out in the open a few blocks from the museum where he was intended to finally arrive.

The Master saw the flashing lights and all the effort to protect what was inside, as the five scrolls was what he had been after. The Master was ready for a fight, and he certainly prepared himself in expectation of one. All the police had been drawn to the museum and the Triads were the first line of defense to stop him. The streets were clear, and the papers that had been blowing through the destroyed areas of the city rustled through the smoke and the fire. There was a palpable feeling in the air of impending doom and destruction.

Everyone had been notified via the radios that this was it, and The Master had come out of hiding. The Master stood with his body armor and his two swords, while the Triads and the rest of the police that hadn't been there raced forward upon hearing that The Master was there.

Matt, Captain Thomas, and the rest of the reinforcements had rushed to get there to try to protect the museum. Matt attempted to get there as fast as he could, as Captain Thomas had received the same radio call. The Triads were all covered in black and had cloaks on as well. They steeled themselves in preparation to defend the city against the mighty Master.

As the group of fifty surrounded the area, and a burning and a darkened feeling emerged, The Master stood completely still, stoic and unmoving, as the army of police officers stood behind the Triad group. Why they were attempting to stop him, with the weapons they had, was beyond Matt. But he was encouraged to see that Curtis walked with them, and Tonya, as the leader of the group. As Captain Thomas had already known, if anyone could succeed in slowing him down, this would serve to buy them time as well.

The Master walked very slowly, while the Triads had all taken off their black cloaks and unveiled the code symbol for the Triad group that they all wore across their chest.

The Master moved towards them, holding his two swords in his hands, a dangerous warrior's eyes fixed on the group approaching him. He was in attack mode, which was a deadly sign; there was nothing more dangerous in the world.

He ran at the Triad group, and the fight for the city was on. The Master had no fear, not of a single one of them. Truly, he had no fear of getting attacked, as there was nothing that The Master had ever feared. He looked at them as a threat to his world, which he was still living in from that of 400 years ago.

The Master saw them, and as they all ran to attack the same enemy, he dove into the group and knocked them all down with a brute force that was unmatched by any living human.

The Master stood up and quickly went to work. His movements were faster than anyone, and strategizing an attack mode, or even a slight attempt to hit him with anything wasn't an option. The Master jumped on top of cars, using his agility to his advantage. His hands and feet were weapons, along with his skillful mastery of his swords.

The Triads, despite their great number, couldn't attempt to protect the museum either. The Master's ability thwarted even their greatest skills.

The Master swung his sword, and the bodies of the Triad group dropped one by one. Each kill was more vicious than the next, and no one realized how deadly the master was. He killed like it was as effortless as breathing, like it was all he had truly known. It was the only thing that he had focused on in his training.

The Master threw bodies into burning fires and used his surrounding environment and the objects around him as a weapon or a means of evading his pursuers, leaping around cars, buildings, then picking up and flinging objects that were strewn about the streets.

Each kill was bloodier than the last, and soon after each swipe, his sword began to be caked full of blood that seemingly covered the old blood from 400 years ago, which had left stain marks on his sword from so long ago.

The Master's body count kept growing, and the police just watched in anguish, as they knew he wasn't going to be stopped by the Triads. Matt could barely look; the death of the entire Triad squad was a hard thing to watch, and now his attention was turned to Curtis. The Master grabbed him around the waist, slammed him down into surroundings cars, and tossed him around.

As much as Curtis did to fight back, and the body shots that some of the Triads who were left standing inflicted on The Master, it wasn't enough to stun him yet. Each shot that they seemingly landed lasted all of about thirty seconds. Curtis let go of him and slammed into the side of an old rusted Chevrolet.

Curtis went after him with whatever Triads had been left from the attack. One of the Triads had been in a burning car—a Hummer—and drove it right towards The Master, aiming towards where Curtis was. As Curtis moved out of the way, his fellow Triad smashed the Hummer into The Master, pushing him right through a coffee shop. The vehicle smashed right through the building.

As the Triad stumbled out of the car and looked around, not seeing where The Master was at all, with all the debris from the crash at the velocity of the impact, the Triad was lucky to have not gone through the windshield himself. With the load of debris that was covered in the Hummer as well, it had made it very difficult to move or even step with everything that had been destroyed in the coffee shop as well.

The Triad group that had been left standing or not completely destroyed by The Master looked on, stunned. The one Triad who had gotten out of the car, had looked for The Master and hadn't seen him. As he looked, and the others had turned around and searched as well, he saw the others come to help him look for the Master.

The Triad felt a nudge on his foot as something was caught on it, but as he looked up, it wasn't that at all. It was The Master. He had lain under the Hummer and used his right arm to cut upwards. In one smooth slicing motion, The Master had cut the body of the Triad in half, and all the fighter's organs spilled out onto the ground.

Unwittingly, the other Triads came to where The Master had been hiding, but they couldn't find where he was in the small building. The Master dropped down and as the building was still standing by a thread, The Master brutally killed the remaining triads, using his swords and his strikes from his hands and feet. It was a gruesome scene, and body parts were flung across the teetering building's shaky frame, raining down amongst the other rubble. This succession of kills was particularly bloody and fierce.

The Master had killed all of the Triads—almost. Tonya and Curtis were left, and now it was a free for all, as the guns had been fired by the police towards The Master, and it had done nothing to affect him at all. As Curtis had run to fight The Master, he and Tonya exchanged a glance and a hopeful nod, knowing they would give it their best shot but fearful of the outcome.

Tonya ran towards him and jumped at him, and just as quickly, The Master had caught her and threw her out of sight like a person throwing an unwanted doll across a room. He threw her so far that Curtis lost sight of how far she had gone.

Curtis limped to get to The Master for having abused his wife. He was still hurting as much as ever, and he knew he couldn't stand one punch from The Master or it would be the nail in the coffin for his fight. He was sore and could barely stand, and meanwhile, the other police officers had stopped firing in order to not hit Curtis or his wife.

The Master looked at Curtis and went ballistic, nearly beating the life out of Curtis with a quick combination of martial arts maneuvers, using his hands and feet, and Curtis had no business trying to resist. No one really had a chance, as he was far superior than anyone else at his trade.

The Master dropped him carelessly, then relentlessly punished him with hard kicks and punches that couldn't keep anyone standing toe to toe with The Master. He was much too big, too strong, and too powerful. There was nothing that Curtis could have withstood, since he kept hitting the leg of Curtis, which was his weak point. Curtis collapsed.

Now that The Master stood before the museum, the bodies of all the dead Triads scattered around at his feet, there was nothing left for The Master to do except get those scrolls he wanted and coveted. It was all about what he had lost in coming down Okla mountain so many years ago.

This was something that had signaled an object that held meaning to The Master.

The Master had killed so many of the Triads, police officers, and others, as the body count rose, and the blood on his sword encased it in an even thicker layer of gore. Thrusting his hands through people's bodies, and killing with such skill, the sight of the red-eyed warrior was frightful. The Master had and was a killing machine. He didn't care who or what was in his way.

Chapter 10

The Master stood in front of the large entrance to the Museum of Natural History. As Matt looked on and glanced at Sherry, they both sprinted towards the main entrance of the museum. Sherry had a head start. They all knew that the sight of what was about to happen outside the museum could be a blood bath.

Matt and Sherry got to the entrance of the museum and walked inside.

Captain Thomas looked at them both, and they knew something was happening. Captain Thomas gave them a meaningful look.

"Find the scrolls and protect them," he said vehemently.

Sherry had the urn in her hands. Now it was only up to Matt and Sherry to provide a line of defense for the city.

The guards stood at the entrance like they were going to be the ones who would stop The Master. How in the world would they begin to attempt to stop The Master? The barricade of police had every gun and every type of weapon in their hands, and each of those could have been something that would have attempted to stop The Master. A barricade of cars had blocked the paths of the pathway to the museum.

Each step that he had taken, each bit of ground he covered brought him closer and closer to what he wanted. He moved towards the police officer, and it seemed as if the entire city had lined up to stop him. He walked slowly and deliberately, every step purposeful, as if he knew where he was going.

The bullets were flying as the entire police department had lined up like a firing squad, but there wasn't one bullet that had hit him, ricocheting off the solid armor that he wore. A waste of bullets, the police realized, as they repeatedly bounced off his armor that he wore. His gleaming skull and his piercing eyes never flinched.

The Master was the one person who had the ultimate power of his scrolls. He was taking a last stand, in order to gain them, and as they moved, he reacted with agility, trying to avoid the onslaught and attack. But the officers found with dismay that bullets had no effect on The Master at all.

The more bullets had were aimed at him, the angrier he became. He seized and threw damaged cars, or whatever he could find to hurl towards where the cops stood. Meanwhile, the police force created a tight circle around the Master, drawing nearer to him.

He was launching everything and anything as killing plenty of cops through his catapulting the large objects at them. Some of the cops were able to dodge the impact, but others were not so fortunate and suffered an untimely and brutal deaths under the crushing weight of the cars and debris thrown by The Master.

The Master had seen the blood from some of the different men and woman that tried to stave off defeat. The more that they fought and shot, the more they wasted their gunfire. The Master knew that each step he took brought him closer to his goal, and his intensity was reflected in the increasing redness in his eyes. The bullets had wasted their purpose, failing to stop him. The warrior became even angrier, evident by his body language and stride.

It was time, as there weren't any marks or effect rendered by the bullets that had fired from the police officers' weapons. They saw that each bullet had bounced off of him, like nothing could deter him or his course.

The Master stood, more annoyed from each shot that had hit him. With his two swords in his hands, as trustworthy and secure as he knew they were, he knew how to use them and what they could do to defend him. Not even the most dangerous villain could come close to his skill, and not even any of the UFC fighters or the Triads could have stopped him with the swords that they had in their hands either.

The Master approached, and as so many of the cops charged him, one by one he dismantled them from every swipe, one after the other, after the other. As each one confronted him in their effort to stop him from entering the museum, it became apparent that there was no hope. The police officers began to run in all directions.

It was like a battlefield and the fight went on for what seemed like hours. The longer it went on, the more vicious it became in favor of The Master. Matt and Sherry had looked out upon the carnage and the decimation of the police force of Manhattan. It was unlike anything that they could have ever imagined. Bodies, blood, and guts lined the streets, broken bodies were everywhere, no matter which way you looked; it was a disgusting view and smell. Even at night, it was a smell that not many could take without retching.

The burning sensation of The Master's swords cutting right through the flesh of the bodies that he had killed was palpable. There was no hero in this battle. The blows to the bodies were so brutal that the entire police force had been eliminated from start to finish. Around the entire museum, all bodies had been scattered—a pile of what seemed like hundreds and hundreds of dead UFC warriors, Triad fighters, and anyone who had the courage to attempt to stop him from obtaining the five scrolls of terror.

The Master stood with his bloodied armor and his swords that had been caked in gore, and his face that was all silver and had blood smeared from the battle. He had singlehandedly destroyed and killed everyone that was in his path. How in the world was someone like him ever going be stopped? There was nothing that could have stopped this invincible warrior from killing people as easily as he was. Not a single person who had tried to stop the Master was left alive.

Matt and Sherry had stood there as Captain Thomas was outside of the museum, and they knew that he was going to try to stop him, as it was in his nature to take a stand that way.

Matt ran down towards where the entrance to the museum was. The Master saw Matt looking at him, as Captain Thomas fired directly and hit him numerous times. As before, the bullets didn't affect him.

Captain Thomas stood in front of The Master. In a moment of clarity, he knew that his fate was death. He looked at Matt. His other son was in the hospital recovering from the beat-down of The Master.

The Master looked at the father of two with hatred. He flung something at Captain Thomas, rendering him immobile, while Matt tried to take the gun away from The Master, as he had cornered him.

The Master crawled forward, as Matt ran down the stairs. Sherry tried to hold onto Matt but quickly, she couldn't hold onto her boyfriend any longer. She had seen the look in the eyes of The Master and knew that he only harbored ill will for the man.

As Matt looked on helplessly, The Master hit the back of Captain Thomas's spine with the pole that held ropes together for line control. He slammed the back of the black man's spine over and over, causing great pain.

Captain Thomas couldn't walk from the impact. He held himself in a fetal position, as The Master kicked his body rapidly, and Matt watched. The more he yelled at The Master, the more and more punishment The Master gave his father.

The older man's upper body was bleeding badly, and he could barely move but tried his best to crawl. The Master saw him try to grab the pole of the column and pull himself up, but he was too weak even to do that.

The Master seized the opportunity, walked over toward him, and smashed the front of his head into it. The Master saw the teeth fly out of Captain Thomas's mouth upon impact.

Matt fell to the floor, and could barely watch as The Master raised Captain Thomas off the ground, lifting him with one finger. The Master slammed his fist into the man's helpless form and looked into the eyes of Captain Thomas. His own eyes burned in their sockets. With a menacing sneer, he looked at him, punched him right in the heart, and ripped his heart right out of the chest of Captain Thomas.

Matt's father fell to the ground. The Master threw the heart right on top of his body.

The Master moved to the entranceway and punched the door down, shattering it from the door frame. Matt gave him a long stare, and he ran as fast as he could. Sherry was on the second floor, trying to find the Japanese part of the Museum of Natural History.

Matt sprinted towards the staircase, where Sherry was. He quickly scaled the staircase up to the second floor, where Sherry stood. Seeing The Master press onward, slowly and confidently, evoked fear in them while they both looked down at him. It urged them to increase their speed.

In the museum, most of the security guards had run off long before The Master was at the door to the museum. Meanwhile, Sherry had seen the map of the museum and read it on the little stone that they had anchored on the second floor. Matt looked at her and grabbed her hand.

"We need to run," he said.

As they ran, she clutched the Urn of Symboltos tightly, which she had taken from Curtis and Tonya when the pair had been tossed aside and rendered vanquished in the fight against The Master earlier. Now Sherry had it, and she held it in one hand while she held Matt's hand in the other. They ran for dear life.

The Master had progressed his steady pace up the stairs where Matt and Sherry had been, and they hadn't yet had time to look for the scrolls that The Master was seeking.

Matt and Sherry both wondered what the hell was so important about those scrolls, especially if he was immortal. They needed to find out.

"What do you think their power is?" Matt asked.

"Beats me, but we'd better locate them soon," Sherry said with urgency.

Matt and Sherry had finally reached the room with all the exhibits to represent Feudal Japan. They walked around the room, looking from exit to exit at the things just in case they had missed it. There were several small exits in the room.

Sherry stopped in a room before the prehistoric dinosaurs. It had a bunch of Japanese warriors and artifacts, but it had no identification on the archeologists who had found them. It was the scrolls that she had found. There was a tiny letter next to them, which was rolled up. She took the back of her gun and smashed the end against the glass, partially shattering it.

They knew the alarm was about to go off, alerting The Master that the scrolls had been found. Matt looked at his red-haired girlfriend. He nodded, urging her to go ahead and do it.

She smashed the glass again, shattering it into pieces, exposing the contents: some little letters on paper, all in Japanese. It looked as if it had been written 400 years ago.

The strange symbols were clearly not from the modern era. Matt knew they didn't have much time.

Matt reached over and grabbed the scrolls as he stepped forward and sorted through the broken glass. Matt grabbed the scrolls, and as soon as he did, they could hear the steps of the warrior approach. Matt seized the papers, and he ran with it, as Sherry did as well. They barely had time to get out of the room as the alarm sounded, resulting in security devices shutting down the exits to the museum, bars locking in place along the different rooms of the museum.

Matt and Sherry had to get out of that room and figure out another way out of the museum.

The Master saw the glass shining, broken into bits, and then he saw the bars. With a derisive snort, he looked at them and bent the bars, breaking the entire gate in one easy motion, snapping it apart.

Matt and Sherry looked at each other, wondering what had just happened. They really didn't want to hesitate in order to find out.

The Master looked and saw the exhibit, along with the language that was a bit more current then his 400-year-old language that he knew. He was angry as he began to read the exhibit and saw what he had read. Anger and frustration appeared on the Japanese warrior's face.

He seized a pole and threw it with force into one of the other Japanese exhibits, destroying the glass. The alarm blared, and he was getting even more enraged hearing the alarm, so quickly, he located it and smashed it to pieces as well, after ripping the wires right out of the wall and caving in part of the wall. He threw the alarm across the room, flinging the red bell and destroying one other glass case in the process.

Matt and Sherry could hear the noise and then heard how the alarm had stopped buzzing. The silence unnerved them, as they had a feeling that it was The Master and that there was no one capable of doing that but him. It seemed as though Matt and Sherry didn't have the strength of The Master, nor the skill either. Now they were trapped. The alarm was broken and the bars had sealed the rest of the museum off, leaving them no way of leaving the museum.

Matt and Sherry were running out of places to run, and they needed to find a way out, soon. Frantically, they searched, but each door they found was either locked or sealed completely shut. Even with the limited gunfire that each of them had, there wasn't much they could do. They really didn't want to use any of the bullets that they had in order to try to stop The Master, as they had seen already firsthand that bullets didn't do anything against him. They had little recourse left, and they were locked inside of a cage, hopeless, with no chance of getting out.

Matt looked at her, panic-stricken. "There has to be a way out of this building," he said.

He saw the door to the roof and gestured.

"Are you crazy?" she said, her voice trembling. She looked up. Then, she looked back down in resignation. Sherry knew it was the only thing that would have worked for the time being. All they had to do now was find the door that led to the roof.

Matt and Sherry began to look for a staircase that might lead to the roof. They always had to have them around someplace, as fire emergencies needed an escape exit per the building's regulations.

Sherry and Matt searched the entire place without running into The Master, incredibly. The Museum of Natural History was a big museum with many different floors. However, they knew that eventually The Master would find them. Matt and Sherry were very mindful of that, and staying alive was their motivating factor not to give up. With so many twists and turns that they had, there was no way they could get up to the roof, but they both began to think of a way of getting far from The Master. That was the end game for them. Going up to the roof would make their fate within reach.

Matt looked at his girlfriend. "Well, neither one of us truly has any great ideas that were passed down to Curtis and Tonya. But this urn wasn't in Mr. Sasaki's hands for no apparent reason. There has to be something behind it."

Sherry thought about that as well. She thought Matt might have been on to something.

"What if there is something about this urn?" she speculated. "Curtis was told about this Urn of Symboltos only when the timing was right. I don't think Mr. Sasaki even understood it. It was something that was passed down to him and his family for so long, but it seemed as if the true power of the urn was mostly heresay to him. But there must be some magic about it."

The Master had walked to the other side of the room where the five scrolls of terror had been taken by Matt and Sherry. He walked to the other side of the room and, as before, shattered the bars that kept him in the room.

He destroyed the other set of bars on the other side of the room as well.

The Master stepped over the broken bars. The Master was out.

Matt and Sherry heard the bars fall down and the loud noise that had rattled the glass of each display that was around the museum. Some of the glass had broken from the loud noises. Glass and broken artifacts and exhibits had been scattered all around the different parts of the museum. There wasn't any part of the museum that hadn't been touched with destruction. Even some of the precious dinosaur exhibits had collapsed from the vibrating, piercing noise.

Matt and Sherry were able to navigate the museum fairly easily, as they had been there so many times over the years. But Sherry still had to look on the maps from time to time to refresh her memory of where to go. Matt knew that it would only be a matter of time before it might be too late, and they had to hurry to accomplish what they sought out to do.

Matt saw that The Master was now on the second floor, while he and Sherry were on the staircase going up to the third floor, one of the few places that they hadn't explored too much. The Master then began to start talking in a language that only a few would have been able to identify.

The Master saw the legs of Matt and Sherry and had thrown a few daggers at them both, nearly missing Sherry as she climbed the stairs.

They hadn't realized that he was that close to them.

Matt fixed him with a stare, as he held Sherry's hand and they ran up to the third floor. The third floor exhibit was more dinosaurs and things of that nature. There were some cavemen exhibits as well.

Matt looked as they got up the stairs. He and Sherry saw some of the open exhibits that were aired out and not under glass protection. Sherry approached them and grabbed whatever spears that they had as weapons and any other pieces of weaponry that would be useful. At this point, they knew something other than guns would be more than helpful, as bullets had already proved to be ineffectual against him.

Matt saw The Master approach, despite the fact that both Sherry and Matt had been running through the museum trying to remain ahead of The Master. It was limited on where they could run and hide, though, in the Museum of Natural History. So, the idea of them going up to the roof wasn't far off from coming to fruition, as they had nowhere else to go, except the roof.

As the Master had been close behind them, each place in the museum where they thought to go, The Master seemingly had found his way towards them at every turn. They carried a few of the weapons that they had in their hands, and Sherry had the Urn of Symboltos in her hands as well. She knew it was time.

They continued to search for the third floor exit to the roof. With the Master up on the third floor with them, they really were running out of time in order to save themselves. Sherry knew that they had to find the door as quickly as possible. Time was not on their side. They wondered, how hard could it be to find one door to the roof? It had been quite difficult to find, as it was buried off to the side, and it wasn't even a legitimate fire door. It was an exit for employees to access the first floor or go up to the roof. It would have to do, as they really hadn't any other choice.

The Master heard a door close, his senses sharpened. The evil-skulled monster had heard the noise, and he knew he would soon find what he'd been looking for. The couple didn't think to hold the door shut after they'd gone through it so that he couldn't break his way through.

The Master had heard the two people talking, even though they tried whispering. Matt and Sherry thought he was farther away, and not as close as he was.

Now Matt and Sherry had reached the top of the stairs. In a furious gesture, The Master kicked the door down with authority, signaling to them that he was coming.

Both of them ran faster.

Matt had the spear in his hands.

"Do something!" Sherry yelled at him, and her body language spoke enough volumes, as both of them were afraid of the red-eyed skull creature.

Who wouldn't be, no matter how brave the person? Just from looking at him, anyone would have been instantly afraid.

As they shut the door behind them, Matt put the spear through the door handle, then using his handcuffs and her handcuffs around the door, secured the door. They exchanged a meaningful look, as they both knew that this wasn't going to hold that door for long—especially considering that it was night, and pouring rain.

She looked into her bag to examine the urn. "There has to be something about this urn," she muttered.

The Master was headed up the stairs. There was a small, wooden shack that was up on the roof, and Sherry stood under it, as she extracted the Urn of Symboltos from the bag.

She placed it on the ground. The scrolls were in the same bag, along with the letter, which they had no idea how to decipher. It was written on scroll paper that looked as if it would crumble as soon as it was touched. It must have some meaning.

The Master continued to ascend the stairs, as Matt was yelling, trying desperately to find in the pouring rain anything that he could make use of—which wasn't much.

Sherry looked at the paper, and the words on the paper began to glow all in Japanese to English words. It was strange, but as she held the paper, they changed to words that she had some understanding of. It was right before her eyes, and she had to take a double take, not believing what she was seeing. The scroll paper was something that was required in order to release the words on the urn.

Sherry saw the magic work on the scroll paper. She watched as the letters formed and came together, finally becoming words that she could read.

"What's happening?" Matt asked.

Sherry was speechless and wordlessly gestured to the scroll.

The words read: *Free Radagast and the great evil of the world, his family, and curse.* The words weren't anything special; it was simply something reflecting how the story had unfolded, and the role Radagast had played, who had known so much about The Master and where his place in the world and in history was meant to be.

Matt saw a glowing figure amidst a thick cloak of smoke that billowed out from the urn and filled the top of the roof.

Out of the urn came Radagast. Matt and Sherry were in awe at the sight: a very old Japanese wizard stood before them. As soon as the smoke had cleared, the old wizard had fallen to the ground, with his staff at his hands. He looked around at his surroundings, disoriented and mouth agape; he was just puzzled. He had no idea where he was or what was happening.

Sherry looked at him, not knowing what to make of the figure that appeared before her. He looked just as lost and bewildered to see an American woman.

Matt had been yelling as the smoke filled the top of the building, to the point where he couldn't see Sherry from the thickness of the smoke. Matt couldn't tell if it was the clouds from the air, or if it was whatever had been going on with urn that Sherry had been holding. They were only words, and it seemed very hard for Matt to see and compute, as he hadn't physically seen what Sherry had seen transpire and transform with her own two eyes.

Sherry had seen the phenomenon for herself. She now tried to speak words in English to Radagast, but he couldn't understand. The wizard looked at her, perplexed, as she was foreign to him.

Sherry grabbed the paper, and she was hoping that the words she found on the magic paper, which were connected to the urn, would work in the same manner if she read them aloud. Just as the Japanese text had turned to English, perhaps it would work in reverse, but verbally. She held the paper, and as she spoke the words aloud, sure enough, they translated to a language that Radagast could understand.

Sherry held his magic staff and helped him up. She saw that he was weak, and he wouldn't be able to stand by himself.

She finally got him to his feet, and Radagast stood, then started to squint his eyes, as someone who was finally just waking up. Sherry held the paper, and Radagast began to read the paper that they both held onto. It was a scroll paper that had some type of magic on it as well. There was not a lot of time left in which to act, so she had to speak quickly.

She explained as much as she could, with the short amount of time that she had. Sherry described where they were, what century and decade, which made the wizard realize that it had been 400 years since The Master had been frozen.

That was enough that had to be said, and Radagast's eyes lit up. Radagast knew that it was The Master, as Sherry took the five scrolls of terror out of the bag that had the urn. She handed them to Radagast.

Radagast looked at her and smiled. He nodded his head in a gesture of gratitude. As the smoke cleared, Matt ran to Sherry's side.

The Master was punching the door, relentlessly. A few times finally put a hole through the door.

Matt was now standing close beside Radagast, who stood firm.

As the red cloaked wizard looked on, the lightning from the storm provided a reason as to why this was happening. The Master broke down the door, and Radagast's staff became charged up from the lightning. The door came down and The Master stood there, immediately casting his gaze to Radagast, infuriated. The old wizard had frozen The Master, and the two had been equals; now here they were, facing each other again.

The Master charged at him and yelled something in Japanese, which neither Matt nor Sherry could understand.

Radagast shot a bolt of electricity towards The Master, lifting him up with his staff and his electricity. He smashed him into the smoke pipes that were on the roof, then smashed him against various other objects along the way, finally throwing him down the stairs, back through the door that he had come from.

The Master was catapulted through the door and crashed all the way down. The Master finally lay in a heap down on the bottom floor of the museum.

As that had bought some time, Radagast floated up in the air, the powerful of all the wizards. He floated up and then it was revealed in another burst of light that he had brought Takeo with him. Takeo materialized before them, the same shogun who had been killed before, by The Master. The highly decorated shogun was resurrected, all his limbs and body parts intact, crouched beside the wizard. Out of all of them, he was likely the one shogun who had similar skills to The Master, and though he'd been defeated before, he'd learned from his mistakes, and he had always been able to hold his own in battles. He would relish the opportunity to exact revenge for what had happened to him.

Takeo regarded Radagast with gratitude, his shogun armor on—only slightly less than what The Master wore—and his swords in both hands.

Takeo had been kneeling, but once Radagast breathed the name of The Master aloud, it shot through him and made him spring to action. The shogun stood and ran towards the stairs where The Master had gone.

The Master saw Takeo run right towards him. Both fighters readying themselves, they locked eyes in a hateful stare. The Master charged and tackled him through a few different exhibits, while both of them struggled to grip each other, both fighting for control. They both tried to head-butt each other, as neither one of them had their swords in hand at the moment, as they'd been knocked loose and clattered to the floor. Neither one would budge no matter how hard the hits kept coming.

The Master was a harder striker overall, and much stronger than Takeo was. From the onslaught of The Master's pummeling, Takeo finally let go and took a variety of combo kicks and punches that were delivered one after the other.

As Takeo could block some, staying on top of him was key. But The Master was extremely quick, and as soon as Takeo would attempt to move or get to his feet, yet another punishing kick or punch would come right after him.

There was no clear way to beat The Master. Creating space between them was what had to be done. Creating that was easier said than done. As Takeo side-swiped his leg and locked up The Master's arm, he then shifted his body on top of The Master, laying punch after punch after punch, finally making him bleed. The eye of The Master was busted open from the fierce hits that The Master had received. He wasn't used to taking such a beating.

One after another, the blows were exchanged, wicked, strong, and rapid. The Master flipped his opponent off to the right. Takeo ran towards him, facing the caveman exhibit on the first level. The Master was on his feet, and Takeo ran towards him with great speed, trying to catch The Master off guard with a blitz.

He caught Takeo easily and was able to grab the arm of his foe. He threw the 6'0" Takeo right through the glass of the caveman exhibit. Takeo landed on a log and broke it. His breath heaved, and his back arched. He was hurt.

Takeo rolled around after he felt the impact from landing on the log. He lay there for a bit before getting up, and then finally pulled himself up and shook himself off from the impact.

The Master was just getting himself up as well. There were enough places in the exhibit to hide, as the buffalo were big enough in the huge exhibit to create a visual obstruction. The Master had walked towards the spot where he had seen Takeo disappear.

The Master was walking and didn't see where he was, despite looking closely. Just then, hurtling himself over the buffalo, Takeo came jumping and swinging at The Master like a baseball bat. He connected and swung again at The Master, sending him flying through the air about fifteen feet away from him.

Takeo had the two pieces of log broken in half, and he held both pieces in each hand. The Master got up, far from his swords, not aware of where they were.

The Master broke part of the tusk off from one of the buffalo exhibits, and grabbed it fiercely, as The Master and Takeo ran at full tilt toward each other.

As they collided to do battle, each swung at their log and tusk, each trying to kill one another, and each blow harder than the next. The Master and Takeo maintained their balance and their footwork, as crucial as each step was. The strength of each swing danced around the possibility of one to take advantage of the other. The Master and Takeo both kicked each other at the exact same time, knocking each other away from the other.

The Master got up and ran towards Takeo with a knife that he had on his waist, and he jumped on Takeo in a swift movement, trying to force the knife into the skull of Takeo.

Takeo struggled as the blade neared his eyes. The Master slashed the side of Takeo's face as he was then tossed to the side. Takeo wiped the blood off the side of his cheek and saw the blood drip.

Takeo and The Master sprinted at each other, and now neither one of them had any weapons in their hand. They were both rapidly on the receiving end of many alternating power kicks and agile moves, a see saw battle of kicks and blocks and tosses by two fighters who just never knew when to give up or relent. Takeo and The Master had gone back and forth for some time, not one gaining an advantage over the other.

Was the Master truly better than Takeo, or was Takeo merely caught off guard?

Finally, the Master had landed so many powerful moves, and moves that Takeo never saw coming. An onslaught of power kicks and punches demonstrated his quickness that was something that so many had talked about. The speed and the expert maneuvers had shown the likes of most police officers, and UFC fighters, that he was not to be trifled with. For such a small warrior, his intensity was enormous, and it showed his power with the velocity behind those kicks and punches, and one after the other after the other, The Master was landing each one perfectly.

The Master was knocking Takeo all over the marble floor, and the blood that had burst forth from his face, and the pouring marks that he had from the armor that protected him, resulted in a bloodbath as the fists of fury that had left his body marked from the impact of the punches.

Takeo was still moving, little by little, damaged, beaten, and bruised from the hits that The Master had given Takeo. There wasn't anything that he could have done. The Master had seen his mouth spitting up blood, and Takeo's face was all red, but as weak as he still was, he still tried to get up each time. Each time The Master walked near him, Takeo just wouldn't stay down. Takeo was either showing guts… or stupidity. When it came down to it, Takeo never wanted to be defeated by The Master, and he would do anything to stall that conclusion.

The Master had walked over, and from where they were on the floor, he had spotted his swords; he disappeared from the fight. Neither fighter had kept track of even knowing where they had lost their sword to begin with, never mind where to recover them.

Matt and Sherry, meanwhile, had run down the stairs, gasping at the sight of The Master holding up his sword triumphantly, his red eyes and skull gleaming as he stood over Takeo as if he were about to thrust his sword cleanly through Takeo's chest.

Matt saw him, and both of them looked on as they got to the bottom of the stairs where The Master had been, just a few feet away. The Master turned around and caught them both, and then he looked away to ensure that Takeo was still there.

As he bent down to stabilize Takeo before impaling him, Radagast suddenly came flying down, crashing through the ceiling with great force. The Master saw him, but it was too late. The wizard zapped The Master with his magic staff, and a great bright light enveloped them both.

They both disappeared.

#

Matt and Sherry looked at each other, incredulous. The building had been wrecked.

Takeo was severely hurt. The pair lifted him up and called 911, then had him transported to a hospital to help him recover from his injuries.

It had been many days and weeks that had gone by. The city had been mourning the deaths of all the police officers and all the other brave people who had put up a fight against The Master and lost their lives. There was no clear path for the future now, after what was done. What to do with Takeo was one of the lingering questions.

To rebuild the city's police force, the mayor had granted them heavier funding, as requested. Matt became a captain and had taken over his father's precinct that he had run. He had seen his father die trying to stop The Master, and he and Jack had finally put some of the things behind them that had caused their relationship strife in the past. In light of the events, they had both come to realize it was family that meant something to everyone. The years that they had both lost over all the petty issues between them made them realize time was short.

Both Takeo and Jack had been recovering and were released from the hospital weeks after The Master had vanished. It was strange; there was not one sign of where they could have gone. Trying to get to the bottom of that was nearly impossible; they couldn't seem to get an answer, even from Takeo, since he wasn't familiar with English either. Despite some Japanese interpreters having tried to talk with him, spending months trying to help him and get him everything that he needed, the mystery of where The Master had gone remained unsolved.

Matt really wanted someone to teach him English so that they could understand each other. Thankfully, Takeo was a fast learner. Finally, after months and months, Matt could finally speak directly to him without an interpreter, which is what he truly wanted. Matt had taken Takeo under his wing, and in time had even given him a job. Though he was unfamiliar with his surroundings, he had been given a second chance at life. That is what Radagast had given him, and he intended to make the most of it.

It brought a tear to Matt's eye when Takeo was finally able to articulate in English, "Thank you, my new friend."

Takeo never looked back, and he was immensely grateful. The only unfortunate part was that this gratitude was something that Mr. Sasaki would have loved to hear from Takeo.

Takeo was eventually able to give Matt some information, and with Curtis and Tonya present in the room, along with Sherry, he described the things that had happened 400 years ago from his point of view, which was enlightening and brought a new context and understanding to the events that had just recently transpired.

Curtis and Tonya found that there were many things they had not known. As Takeo had warned them, though, The Master wasn't like anyone or anything that was ever seen before. Somehow, he felt that a return was possible. After all, The Master had not died, nor could he with his powers. No one, including Takeo, knew where The Master had been taken by Radagast. It left everyone in the room feeling wary and on edge. Meanwhile, the city had its plan to move forward. Curtis and Tonya had work of their own to do once they returned to Japan as well.

It was approaching Saturday, and it was very close to a year after everything had happened with The Master. Matt had proposed to Sherry weeks after Tonya and Curtis had flown in from Japan, and Jack was his best man, a farfetched notion, but they had come a long way and had bonded. They were much closer now than they had been almost a year ago, the loss of their father having brought them closer together.

Matt and Sherry were to be married at Styptics Cathedral, a wonderful and beautiful church in Manhattan. It was their day, and nothing in the world could have destroyed it.

As the church filled with people, and Matt stood in the front of the church with his brother as the best man, he finally saw Sherry in her white wedding dress. As the wedding song played, Matt stood at the altar, waiting for his beautiful bride to come down the aisle. He smiled, as seeing her was something that he couldn't have waited another second or minute for.

The moment had really hit hard for Matt, as they had been through so much together, and especially considering Sherry had waited for him for what was, up to this point, thirteen years. Finally she would get to marry the man that she had cared so much about for all those years.

She cried, as both Sherry's parents had been deceased five years prior. They both had pictures of both of their parents up at the altar, as all of them had been dead, but never forgotten.

Matt grabbed her hand as she reached the front of the altar. She smiled, as the tears of such an emotional feeling she shared with Matt prompted her to cry in both happiness and sadness, happy to be marrying Matt, but wistful that her mother and father were not there to see it. She saw Matt crying as well, and she was sure he was thinking the same thing. They shared a tight embrace, as they prepared to become husband and wife.

As the priest began to say the mass, Matt felt a very disturbing presence. Sherry gave a look of concern, indicating she had felt something as well. Matt had looked from Sherry to the people filling the seats, and that was when he saw someone standing in the back of the church.

It was The Master, who knew Matt would see him eventually. The warrior lifted the hood of his cloak to reveal his face, then swiftly put the hood back up to conceal his face as he left the church.

"Did you see that?" asked Sherry. "Was it him?"

"It was," said Matt.

They ran down the church steps. As they did, they caught sight of a military truck going by. What they didn't know was that the truck had been transporting a robot named Nemesis, and its route happened to be going by the church.

They searched everywhere, but they couldn't locate where the menacing cloaked figure had gone. Never would they have thought that he might have taken advantage of the convenient transportation that had presented itself.

The Master was in the back of the military truck with Nemesis. All the guards were instantly and efficiently killed. Then, after dispatching them, he closed the back of the van with Nemesis inside. It was a whole new world, and The Master had come back to life, through his prevailing powers of immortality.

The Master, as it turned out, had killed Radagast, once he had been taken to the Temple of Time, and he had also killed all eight of the wizards of time. Now, somehow, he had returned to the world that was New York, and the universe that only those wizards had known.

The Master was alive and breathing.

As they had been warned, legends never die; they only begin.

THE END